THE OXFORD MURDERS

A gripping crime thriller full of twists

PETER TICKLER

Doug Mullen Mystery Book 4

JOFFE BOOKS

Joffe Books, London
www.joffebooks.com

First published in Great Britain in 2023

© Peter Tickler

Cover art by Nick Castle

ISBN: 978-1-80405-871-8

PROLOGUE

I found the business card in the inside pocket of his striped suit jacket, the one with a red lining. He thinks I am pretty useless now, but I like going through his dirty clothes, checking he hasn't left anything in the pockets. That is something I can do for myself on a good day. It is Ngung's job to do the rest — wash, dry, iron, sort out the dry cleaning — but when my head isn't full of fuzz, doing the simple things makes me feel useful.

Sometimes, of course, I come across things I would rather not have found, condoms for example, or the empty packet of one, but never an actual used condom — ugh, that would be too horrid! Ngung tells me to focus on the nicer things. Only the other day I found a half-eaten packet of mints in the pocket of his blue chinos, and a few weeks ago I found an unopened chocolate bar in his jacket pocket. I told Ngung about it and we shared it for elevenses. We both agreed he wouldn't notice.

As for the business card, that was different. It read, "Private Investigator." When Ngung realized what a private investigator was — 'It's like that man on the TV with one leg,' *I told her — she became alarmed.* 'We must put it back,' *she said,* 'before he comes home. He will be cross.'

I wasn't sure why he would get cross, but when he does, it isn't nice at all. I don't like to see Ngung upset, so I said straight away that I would put it back in the jacket pocket, and she could give it a really

1

good brush and press the trousers too, and then we would hang it back in its place and he would know nothing about it. But while she brushed the suit and sponged a mark off one of the lapels, I did something a bit naughty. I wrote down the private investigator's name and phone number very carefully in a little notebook I kept hidden in my special box. Then I gave the card to Ngung to put back in the jacket pocket. I didn't tell her what I had done. She might have stopped me if I had. But as my poor mother used to say, you never know when something will come in useful.

CHAPTER 1

The guy seemed nice, but Julie knew all too well that first impressions can be disastrously unreliable. However, this one really did look OK. His hair was a bit short but his eyes were friendly, and besides, he had her bus pass in his hand.

'You dropped this.' A nice enough voice too. Ordinary, not posh, though she couldn't quite pin it down to a particular part of England.

'Thanks.' She took it from him and stuffed it deep inside her handbag. 'I'd have been stuck without it.'

'Can I buy you a drink?' he said.

She didn't say anything, but he must have seen the alarm on her face because he stepped back and held his hands up in front of him. 'Sorry. Inappropriate.'

She glanced around. The cinema was three-quarters empty. She had arrived early and there was no sign of them dimming the lights for the adverts before the film. She looked back at him, saw his embarrassment and gave the briefest of nods. 'Sorry.' They were both at it now — apologizing. 'Actually, a juice would be nice. But just for the record, I am waiting for a friend.'

'Will he be upset if I . . . ?'

'No!' She blurted the word out. 'He's . . . he's very easy-going.'

They stood together for a couple of minutes, sipping and making awkward conversation, then he moved off to his seat and she to hers.

She found it hard to enjoy the film. She had called in a favour from Bridget to sit with her mother, and as a consequence she had been really peeved when he had texted her — *texted* her for crying out loud — with the message, *Sorry, Julie, something's come up at work. I'll catch you later if I can.* She was already on the bus by then, so there was no going back, and unless he made it up to her later that evening, there would be no second chance for him.

She stood up as soon as the credits began to roll, hot-footed it to the toilets and headed for the exit. If she missed the last bus . . .

'Didn't your friend turn up?' It was him again.

'I'm in a hurry,' she said, but not so much of a hurry that she didn't pause and see what else he had to say for himself. Had he been waiting for her?

'Do you need a lift home?'

Don't be so stupid as to accept a lift from a man you don't know. Her mother's words, drummed into her from adolescence, rang in her ears, but not very loudly. After all, it was some twenty years since she had first been offered these words of advice. At the time, they had been sensible, and in the beginning she had followed them. But what constituted a stranger? A student you have just met in a bar? A middle-aged man in a crumpled suit who has kindly offered to buy you a kebab from a fast-food van? A grey-haired academic type who has engaged you in conversation during the interval of a gritty new play at the Old Fire Station? But this stranger is none of these, and yet, perhaps because he is a man, he could be all of them.

He stands there waiting for a reply. So she gives him one.

'No thanks.'

The stranger shrugs and looks up as the rain begins to fall. 'Where are you headed? Because I don't mind going out of my way. My mother taught me that.'

So it is a case of his mother versus her mother. Whose will be the stronger?

* * *

He grabbed her, one hand on the collar of her coat, the other tugging fiercely at her buttons.

'I said, "No!"'

'I say, "Yes!"'

She yelled and he swore. In the dark she felt an explosion of pain as his hand smashed against her cheek. Then his right hand was under her blouse, forcing its way under her bra and grasping greedily at her breast. She would have been raped there and then, and maybe that would have been the terrible beginning and end of it, but she refused to submit.

'OK,' she squealed. 'OK, I'll let you do it but, please, if my clothes are torn my mother will notice and then there'll be hell to pay.'

To her amazement, he paused, moved back a little, lifting his weight away from her. 'You'd better not be . . .'

He never finished his sentence, because with every ounce of strength she had, she brought her knee hard up into his groin, kicked his stomach with her other leg and grabbed for the door handle.

Seconds later, she was running, her coat flapping open, terror and adrenaline powering her across the field. She had been a good runner at school, coming third in the cross-country in her final year, but running in three-inch heels across a rain-softened field of winter wheat is not easy, and the man was gaining on her. She heard his heavy panting, the occasional curse and then, quite suddenly, she tripped and fell. She struggled to her feet but he was upon her and she knew that something terrible was going to happen to her. She knew too that there was nothing she could do to prevent it.

* * *

Julie never made it home to her mother. Never relieved Bridget. Never knew of the panic her disappearance engendered in them both. However, there was no such panic at Thames Valley Police when Bridget rang at 1.30 a.m. to report that Julie Baxter had failed to come home after a date.

'Women often fail to come home after a date,' she was told. 'She's probably gone home with him.'

'She would have rung me! I'm looking after her disabled mother.'

'Maybe she lost track of the time.'

'But she's not answering her phone!' The calmer the woman from Thames Valley Police remained, the more distressed Bridget grew.

'She's probably left it on silent. She'd have done that for the film, wouldn't she?' The super-calm call handler had an answer for everything.

'So what am I meant to do?'

'I suggest you ring us back in the morning if she still hasn't returned. But most likely she'll turn up on your doorstep at the crack of dawn, all apologetic.'

But Julie didn't turn up at the crack of dawn — it was halfway through the afternoon. And she didn't turn up on the doorstep, apologetic and looking the worse for wear. Instead, she turned up at the bottom of a ditch a couple of miles outside Oxford.

It was Keith Daynes who found her while out walking with a shotgun under his arm. The gun was unlicensed as it happened, but Daynes received credit for ringing it in and remaining next to the body until two PCs turned up in a marked police car. They were followed shortly afterwards by a pair of paramedics in an ambulance, a scene-of-crime team and, immediately behind them, two detectives — DS Andy Kingston and DC Jim Royce — in an unmarked car. The detectives lumbered as fast as they could across the field to get a first look while the others were getting themselves organized.

'Bloody hell!' Kingston was a hard-nosed man with a face that betrayed over ten years of club rugby as open side prop forward. So he was no wilting violet, but what he saw at the bottom of the ditch made him blench. Sometimes he wondered how much longer he could put up with the job, but it paid the bills and the maintenance, and enabled him to go along and watch the football at the Kassam Stadium from time to time, and have a good night out when he wanted it.

'Who the hell could have done that?' Royce lifted a hand to his mouth as if he might be about to vomit, but the moment passed. Instead, he leaned forward, craning to get a better look, and before anyone knew it, his feet had slipped from under him and he was shouting and falling at the same time, arms flailing as he dove forward and came to rest on top of the dead woman.

'What the hell are you doing?' someone bellowed from behind them. Kingston glanced behind him, recognizing Frank Dickens, the pathologist. He was a short man, lean, with metal-rimmed glasses and grey hair clipped close to his skull. Normally, he was helpful and calm, but not on this occasion. He came to a halt beside Kingston and glared down into the ditch where Royce was struggling to stand up. 'Get the hell out of there. That way,' he snarled, pointing along the ditch. 'This is my crime scene and I want you pair of clowns out of it.' He then turned his ire on the uniformed constables. 'You're meant to secure the scene of crime. Where's the tape?'

Kingston sent the mud-bespattered Royce back to the car while he waited for Dickens to calm down. Five minutes later, the pathologist appeared from out of the ditch, and when he saw Kingston still there, barked, 'Well? What the hell are you waiting for?'

'A quick summary, if you don't mind.' Kingston was turning on the politeness.

'A quick summary would be that she's dead. Very nastily dead. Battered to death with something — a sizeable lump of stone, I would guess. She has been dead for a number of hours, so late last night or early morning.' Dickens paused and bent down low, hands on knees, his breathing thick and heavy. Eventually, he straightened up and saw that Kingston was still standing there. 'That's your lot until I get her out of this god-forsaken place. Now beat it.'

'Was she sexually assaulted?'

'I repeat, Sergeant. That's your lot.'

'I assume you've not found a wallet or any form of ID on her?'

Dickens swore. 'I'd have told you if we had, wouldn't I! No ID as yet. No wallet, no handbag. We've not yet checked for name tags on her knickers, but given that she is not a schoolgirl, I doubt there will be.'

'Thank you, Frank. Just one more thing. It would be extremely helpful if you or one of your team could text me details of her clothing soonest. Then we can see if they match anyone who has been reported missing.'

'Very well.' Dickens's ire subsided somewhat. Though he had had enough of Kingston's questions, he appreciated the reasoning behind them. If he had been in Kingston's place, he would have asked them too.

Kingston nodded, still in damage limitation mode. 'Thank you, Frank, you have been most helpful. And sorry about my idiot colleague.'

He turned away and had walked several steps when Dickens called after him. 'Andy!'

Kingston turned round.

'One thing that might interest you. We did find a piece of paper in her coat pocket. It is relevant, I think, to last night.'

* * *

Kingston and Royce had hardly got back to their open-plan office before they were summoned into DI Susan Holden's domain. It wasn't exactly spacious but it was hers, and private. Neither man knew her well, though she had something of a reputation at the station. After a six-month leave of absence — according to the station grapevine she had been

8

stupid enough to let loose her famed temper on the chief superintendent — she had reappeared at the Cowley station one morning, unexpectedly and without explanation.

She glared up at them. 'What exactly are you doing here?'

Kingston was genuinely surprised at the sharpness in her voice. 'We've been out to the scene of crime near Wheatley. There's a dead woman in the bottom of a ditch.'

'A very nasty murder by the look of it,' Royce chipped in, and immediately regretted it because Holden lasered him with her eyes.

'A very nasty murder. Well, well, well. I suppose that is all I need to know, is it? That there's been a *very nasty* murder on my patch.'

'We don't have an identification,' Royce said quickly, trying to recover the situation. 'If the woman had a handbag, her attacker must have taken it—'

'Attacker? She wasn't attacked, she was killed! We are looking for a murderer!'

Holden fell silent. She began to drum her fingers on the desk. Her nails were varnished a soft red, but they were cut short. Kingston wondered if she bit them.

'A few minutes ago, I received a phone call from Frank Dickens. He is very upset by the fact that two of my detectives went blundering all over his crime scene.'

'Blundering is an exaggeration, ma'am,' Kingston said. 'We got there first and were trying to get a look at the victim and—'

'And one of you was stupid enough to fall into the ditch on top of the dead woman. In my book, that would be a perfect example of "blundering."'

'It was just an accident, ma'am,' Royce said. 'It was very slippery and—'

'You were too close. You shouldn't have been there. You should have kept your distance. If you want me to recommend you for a transfer to traffic duties, then you are going the right way about it.' She switched her gaze back to Kingston. 'I will ask you again, Andy, why are you here?'

'I'm not quite sure what you mean, ma'am.'

'I understand there was a cinema ticket in her pocket. So, let me put it in very simple words. Why are you here in the station when you should be at the cinema finding out everything you possibly can about the poor woman?'

'I'm not sure the cinema will be open yet.'

'The first film starts in just under an hour. Are you seriously planning to delay your interview until such time as people are queuing down the street? If the manager isn't there by now, he damned well will be soon.'

'Yes, ma'am.'

'And, Detective Constable Royce, take your filthy clothes off and put them in an evidence bag. Now!'

Kingston and Royce didn't give vent to their feelings until they were in their car and heading for the cinema on Cowley Road. It was only a mile or so but plenty long enough for a sharp exchange of views.

'If I ever meet that Frank Dickens in a dark alley,' Royce began, 'he'd better have his running shoes on.'

'You can't blame him.'

'He rang Susan bloody Holden up and told tales on us.'

'On you, not us.' Kingston had already decided that allying himself too closely to Royce might not be such a good idea.

'Ah, I get it, you're scared of her. Don't want to upset madam, do we?'

'It was your stupid fault. I'm not going to take the blame for it.'

'I'll remember that,' Royce muttered, softly, but not so softly that Kingston couldn't hear.

'What you need to remember,' Kingston snapped back, 'is that I am a sergeant and you are not. Which means that when we reach the cinema, I will ask the questions, you will take notes and otherwise make sure you don't cock things up again. Is that clear?'

* * *

Royce parked the car in Jeune Street. To the left was a church, and on the low wall in front of it two men and a woman were sitting smoking. Opposite, on the other side of the road, was the extraordinary Ultimate Picture Palace, an Art Deco gem of a cinema, complete with half-pillars supporting the front of the cream-coloured building.

The two men got out and made their way to the small ticket kiosk, which was positioned proudly in the middle of the building. There was no sign of anyone there, though there was a bicycle locked up immediately to the left of it. Kingston tapped firmly on the glass, but to no effect. Meanwhile, Royce walked over to a door on the right and, to his surprise, found it open. 'Sir,' he said, now on his best behaviour.

Inside there were lights on low, but no one was visible. The walls were a dark red, the atmosphere intimate. Kingston preferred the more open modern design of the Vue complex out near the football stadium, but even he had to acknowledge that the Ultimate Picture Palace had a charm of its own.

'Hello there!' His stentorian voice echoed round the auditorium.

There was a sound at the far end of the building, then a gleam of white light as a man appeared from, it seemed, under the ground. 'We aren't open for another twenty minutes, I'm afraid. Got to clean and sanitize the toilets and get the bar ready.'

'We're not here to watch a film,' Kingston said firmly as the man approached. 'We are the police and we're here to investigate a death.' And he held up his ID to prove his point.

'So how can I help?' The manager — who had admitted to being Ross Fairfield — had retreated to the small bar at the back of the auditorium and was perched on a stool. He had opened a bottle of orange juice for himself, the two detectives having turned down the offer of a drink.

'We are interested in a woman who attended your cinema last night. This is her ticket.' Kingston held up his phone close to Fairfield's face.

'We had sixty or so people here for that showing.'

'This shows where she was sitting, right? Or do people just sit where the heck they like?'

'Oh no! People get upset if someone sits in their seat. We have a strict policy on that. Especially as some of our regulars always like to have the same seat.'

'We estimate she was in her late twenties, maybe early thirties. Tight-fitting jeans, little black ankle boots, grey blouse, a silver puffer jacket, medium length hair.'

Fairfield was silent. He seemed to be having trouble breathing, and there was alarm in his eyes.

'And this woman is dead, like . . . like she's been murdered?'

'Can you just answer my questions?' Kingston said firmly.

Fairfield took a swig of his orange juice as if it were a beer and he needed it for courage. He looked from one man to the other.

'For crying out loud,' Royce snapped. 'There can't have been that many women in silver puffer jackets here last night!'

Finally, Fairfield opened his mouth to speak, and once he had started the words flowed out unstoppably. 'She was one of the first in for that performance. Attractive woman, slight, hair that she kept brushing out of her eyes. Not a regular, I don't recall seeing her before, but then I am not here every night, and besides, women are always changing their looks, aren't they? A new colour and a new style every time they go to the hairdresser, you know what I mean?'

'Did she buy a drink?' Kingston said, trying to steer the man's recollections. 'Did she speak to you?'

'Well, yes. Or rather, no. I mean, look, this other guy did. I think she must have dropped something, because he picked it up off the floor and gave it to her. And then he came up to the bar and bought a couple of drinks and they chatted a bit and—'

'Did they sit together?'

He frowned. 'No. I'm pretty sure they came in separately, bought their own tickets, so they would have sat in their allocated seats—'

'What about when the film had finished?' Kingston was like a bloodhound that had picked up a particularly exciting scent. If the cinema had CCTV, then maybe they would get a shot of the two of them leaving together. Hell, Holden would have to be pleased with them then.

Fairfield frowned and took another sip of his juice. 'I was kind of clearing up at the end. When people are arriving, you keep an eye open for people with seating problems or wanting to buy drinks and snacks. That's very important for the economics of a place like this. But at the end, it's clearing up the mess, checking the toilets, that sort of thing.'

'So you've no idea?'

'I didn't say that.' Fairfield was getting pretty annoying. 'I think they did. Briefly. She'd been in the toilet, and he was hanging around at the door, but she kind off brushed him off.'

'And did he follow her out?'

Fairfield shook his head, somewhat sadly it seemed, as if it would have been more exciting and made a better story if the man had followed her out, if he had been the murderer, if Fairfield himself was the key witness to an appalling crime. 'Sorry, but monitoring him wasn't top of my agenda.'

'What about CCTV?'

'We have CCTV. But actually I've deleted the files.'

'Already?'

'I did a clear-out this morning because no one had done one for a while.'

'Bloody hell,' Royce snapped again. 'What's the point of having CCTV if you then delete the files?'

'Because nothing untoward happened last night. Nothing untoward ever does. I sometimes wonder why we bother.'

'Any idea where this mystery man was sitting? Did he pay by card? I guess we can identify him that way.'

Fairfield looked from Kingston to Royce to Kingston again, and in that time a distinctly self-satisfied smirk spread across his face.

'I can do better than that.'

He removed himself from his stool, exited the bar and moved over to a board at the back of the auditorium. 'He left this.' He pointed towards a hand-written piece of white card:

Need a House-Sitter? Experienced male available for short-or long-term contract. Good with dogs. References available. Email: DougMullen@MyMail.com

CHAPTER 2

Mullen was wondering how he might tell Becca that he was planning to leave. He had told himself that he would slip it into the breakfast conversation, but somehow he hadn't had the heart to do so. Besides, he had no idea how she would react — with fury at him being so selfish, or with a grunt and a shrug of the shoulders. He wasn't sure which would be worse. Their almost silent breakfast had climaxed with her suddenly looking across the table at him and saying, 'You're cooking tonight then.' It had been a statement, despite being phrased as a question.

'Yes,' he'd replied. It was not his turn, but he was not going to point that out. Admittedly, he had nothing else on that day, but Becca didn't either as far as he knew. The fact was, she still hadn't returned to work, and she never seemed to have anything on. Again, he wasn't going to point that out.

'Good,' she had replied with a finality that made clear that their breakfast small talk was over. She had retreated upstairs for a bath and was still up there an hour later.

For a little while, Mullen remained seated at the kitchen table reading a book he wasn't enjoying and wishing it wasn't raining cats and dogs outside. He would have liked to go for a very long walk with his own dog, but Rex was not an all-weather type, and glancing out of the window, wondering when it would stop, Mullen decided not to drag him off into the deluge.

But he himself was bored. He got up, glad to abandon the book, and went to inspect the fridge and the cupboards. He needed to work out what he could make for supper. And it was while his head was almost literally in the fridge — he had detected a distinctly unsavoury smell in it — that he heard a heavy knocking on the door. He straightened up and went to see if it was the package he had ordered online.

On the doorstep were two men in dark suits, each of them brandishing an ID card. 'Hello. Mr Mullen, I presume? I am DS Kingston and this is DC Royce. Can we come in before we get soaked through?'

Mullen shrugged. He knew a few of the Thames Valley force, but he didn't recognize these two, and perhaps for that reason he didn't offer them coffee or tea. He wondered how they knew he lived here and decided Holden must have told them. Was it possible that the Thames Valley Police needed his services? The thought amused him and cheered him up. The work would be very welcome.

Detective Sergeant Andy Kingston — Mullen had already filed his name and rank away in his head — unleashed a mirthless smile. 'You went to the cinema two nights ago.'

Mullen nodded. 'Yes.'

'Did you enjoy the film?'

'I've seen better and I've seen worse.' He tried to sound nonchalant, but alarm bells were ringing in the distance.

'Perhaps your thoughts weren't fully focused on it?'

Mullen said nothing. He was conscious that the water was gurgling noisily out of the bath above him. There were heavy thuds too as Becca moved around. She would be down soon enough, especially if she could hear them talking.

'Perhaps,' Kingston said, his eyes like those of a king cobra, 'you were thinking about the woman you bought a drink for before the film started.'

Mullen flinched. What the hell had happened? 'I don't understand what this is all about.'

'You did buy a woman a drink before the film?' A long pause. 'Didn't you?'

There was a creak at the top of the stairs. Mullen could sense Becca's eyes on him. 'Yes,' he admitted.

'Would you like to tell us who she was?'

'She didn't give me her name.'

Kingston nodded very deliberately, as if that were precisely what he was expecting to hear. He was, Mullen reckoned, a man executing a carefully laid plan, but his detective constable didn't seem to be aware of this at all. Instead, he jumped in with both his size eleven clodhoppers. 'You seriously expect us to believe that?'

'I expect nothing. I am merely answering your questions.'

'So this woman accepts a drink from you, refuses to tell you her name, and then tells you to beat it. I bet that annoyed you.'

Mullen was normally a mild man, but this made him blaze with anger. He let it show. 'It wasn't like that!'

'Oh yeah?' Royce smirked. Maybe he *was* aware of his sergeant's plan. If they were doing the good-cop, bad-cop routine, then he was playing his part to perfection. 'What was it like, Mr Muggins?'

'His name is Mullen!' Becca snapped from the top of the stairs, before stomping furiously down. She hadn't dressed and her hair was wet and hung tangled over the shoulders of her needlecord dressing gown. 'This is my house, and I want to know who you are and what you think you're doing here.'

'They are police,' Mullen said.

'They can answer for themselves.'

Kingston stepped forward, holding up his ID card. 'Detective Sergeant Kingston of Thames Valley Police. And my colleague is Detective Constable Royce. 'We are investigating the murder of a woman, and we believe Mr Mullen may have been the last person to speak to her before she was killed.'

'Doug?' Becca looked at him and was dismayed to see him nod.

'At the cinema,' he said, in little more than a whisper.

'So we need to ask him questions and—'

'Well, you're not doing that here. You can piss off back to your police station and do it there. And, Doug, you need to have a solicitor with you. I'll ring Althea Potter.'

* * *

Susan Holden would have liked to be in the interview room, taking charge, but she knew that wasn't possible. She and Mullen had "history," not as in one-time lovers or anything like that, but history nonetheless. They weren't exactly friends or colleagues, but there was something between them, an undeniable bond which meant she had to leave the interviewing to Kingston and Royce. And she didn't have much trust in men, Kingston and Royce being no exceptions.

Mullen was on edge, and that bothered her. From what she knew of him, he was the sort of guy who remained calm under pressure, but conferring with Althea Potter, gesturing wildly, face tight with stress, he looked anything but. Potter was a good solicitor to have, but right now she was having a job keeping him calm.

Kingston and Royce came in like some wrestling tag team, pleased with themselves and, in Royce's case, rather cocky. He turned on the recorder while Kingston got the interview underway. He proceeded carefully and unfussily, having clearly worked out his strategy and the questions he needed to ask. Despite her reservations, Holden was impressed. She couldn't fault him, and Royce, she was glad to note, was keeping quiet. But she couldn't help wondering how much of this was down to the fact that they both knew she was observing them.

From Mullen's point of view, the interview was going badly. Yes, he had bought a woman a drink at the cinema. He described her clothes, which corresponded to those worn by the dead woman. He had even admitted to speaking to her after the film and had offered her a lift home, which she had turned down, saying she would catch a bus. He insisted that he had gone straight home after that. At this point, Kingston started to apply pressure, his scepticism becoming perfectly evident.

'So she turned you down a second time? How did that feel? Were you annoyed? Did you follow her out of the cinema and bully her into accepting a lift? Because she never got home. She must have got into someone's car.'

Althea Potter was good too, cutting in and protecting her client. When the interview came to an end, Holden didn't wait but made her way to the balcony from where she could look down on the reception area. As soon as Mullen appeared, the figure of Becca Baines swept forward and with jerk of her head led him outside. Not a word of consolation, no welcoming hug. Holden wondered what the atmosphere in her car would be like. After all, he had admitted trying to pick up another woman. It was hard to know exactly what their relationship was. Was he just a lodger, as he claimed, or were they lovers by now? She suspected the latter.

Holden was still running these thoughts through her head when, a few minutes later, Kingston and Royce appeared at her door. They smelled of cigarette smoke, and both looked pleased with themselves.

'Guilty as sin, if you ask me,' Royce said.

Holden raised her eyes to Kingston. 'You agree, do you, Andy?'

'He's got to be our prime suspect.'

'Early days for a prime suspect, isn't it?' She could feel her anger rising. 'You haven't investigated CCTV. You haven't checked out the other men in the cinema. Who was sitting next to her, behind her, in front of her? Did anyone else speak to her while she was there? Was there someone hanging around at the end of the film?' She paused, catching her breath and trying to catch her temper too. 'Most importantly, we know nothing about this woman or even her name. Check out every misper from the last forty-eight hours. Above all else, we need to know who she is.'

Kingston was chastened, but not willing to lie down. 'Ma'am, he did admit to trying to pick her up.'

'I accept that. But it is possible he was just being nice. Mullen is that sort of guy.'

Holden regretted the words as soon as they were out. They would jump to conclusions, discuss it between themselves, laugh about it down the pub with their mates and colleagues, and eventually the gossip would reach the ears of Detective Superintendent McPherson.

'Yes, ma'am,' Kingston said, his voice as devoid of expression as his face. 'I'll keep that in mind.'

'We need to wait for the forensics too. If, after all that, Mullen remains top of the list, then you have my blessing to pull him in again.'

Without a word, the two men withdrew from her office. *With my blessing?* The words rattled around her head. They felt like a betrayal.

* * *

'I think we may have an ID for the dead woman.' Kingston had appeared in the doorway of Holden's office, hesitant, yet his eyes were gleaming with barely suppressed excitement.

She looked up from her computer and surveyed him. 'Well?'

'A Julie Baxter failed to return home after going out two nights ago. The clothing her neighbour reported her to be wearing matches that of the victim. Hair colour and height, ditto.'

'Does this Julie Baxter have a family?'

'I understand she has a disabled mother who she lives with. But it was a friend who rang it in.'

'You'd better go and see them.'

'Of course.' He paused. 'Jim has gone home sick.'

'Ah.' Thank God. Anyone would be better than that clown. Kingston was hovering, waiting for Holden to pronounce. He was, she suddenly realized, nervous of her, afraid even. Given his size, that seemed ridiculous. She stood up, went to the wall of her cubicle and stared through the large window, scanning the room. 'Better take Krystyna.' A female presence was needed. DC Krystyna Wozniak was inexperienced, but trustworthy.

He nodded.

'Tread carefully. Not that I need to tell you that. But in between, we still need to gather information. Are we looking for someone she knew, or someone she met that night?'

He nodded again and withdrew. Holden watched him go across to the detective constable's desk and speak to her, saw the gleam of pleasure on Wozniak's face, and knew she had made the right decision.

* * *

How do you tell a woman that her missing daughter has very possibly been murdered? Do you tell her that the details she reported, in so far as you have them, tie up with a body found in a ditch outside Oxford? But that it might be someone else, and to clarify it one way or the other you need someone to come and identify the dead woman? What tone of voice do you use? What words? How do you respond when she breaks down, as she surely will? And how do you as a professional but sympathetic officer hold yourself together? How, how, how?

These thoughts and more had been swirling around inside DC Krystyna Wozniak's head all the way from the station to the nondescript 1930s house in Risinghurst that was their destination. Once a small rural village outside Oxford and the home of C. S. Lewis — she had read and loved the *Narnia* books as a child — now it could hardly be described as picturesque, squeezed in as it was between the Thornhill Park and Ride and the Oxford ring road.

'Let me do the talking,' Kingston had said firmly. She had tried not to let her irritation show, but he had, in fact, dealt with a difficult situation with considerable skill and sensitivity. She had sat still, taking notes and listening intently to both the mother, Marjorie Baxter, and her friend, Bridget Moore. Marjorie was wheelchair-bound, and it was Bridget who had come and stayed with her to allow Julie a night out. She had left just after 7 p.m., catching the bus into the city centre.

'And she seemed quite normal?' Kingston asked.

'She was excited to be going out,' Marjorie said quickly. 'When she wasn't working, she was looking after me. I was so pleased for her. She was all dressed up and full of smiles.'

'But you have no idea who she was meeting?'

'She said she was going to meet a girlfriend at the cinema.'

'A girl?'

'A woman. Since she left her bastard of a husband, she hasn't been interested in men.'

'And what is her husband's name?'

'Bob Tapper. She got rid of him and his surname.'

'I see. And where did Julie work?'

'Here, there and everywhere. She's a hairdresser. Runs her own little business, cutting people's hair in their homes.'

'It gives her flexibility,' Bridget added. 'Because of her devotion to Marjorie, she needed that.'

'So she'll have a list of regular clients?'

'Oh yes. She has a red diary with names and addresses and phone numbers, and of course when the next appointment is.'

'May we borrow it?'

'I suppose so.' Marjorie seemed puzzled as to why they might want it. 'Her clients are all ladies, mostly rather elderly I imagine.'

'It's just the way we work,' Wozniak said quickly. 'Don't worry, we will return it.'

'Of course,' Bridget said. 'I think I saw it on the sideboard. I'll go and get it.'

It was also Bridget who insisted on seeing them out a few minutes later, although not for the spurious reason she had given in front of Marjorie: 'I'll check there's no one coming while you're backing out — there was an accident just up the road the other day.'

She shut the front door firmly behind her. 'There's something I haven't said,' she whispered. 'Julie actually asked if I could come prepared to stay overnight. We didn't let on to Marjorie, but I think she had met someone and was hopeful it might lead to something.'

'You mean an invitation to stay over at the man's house? Or something more casual?' Kingston said.

'I'm not sure what you mean by "more casual," Sergeant.' There was a frisson of anger in her voice.

Kingston didn't immediately respond. Perhaps he wasn't used to women of a certain age challenging him.

'It is difficult to ask this of a devoted mother,' Wozniak intervened, 'and, I think, of a very good friend like yourself. But we are hoping to establish whether Julie had an active sex life, perhaps with different men — or perhaps with women.'

'I thought I had just made it clear that this date was important to her. Julie wasn't a slut.'

'I am not a slut either,' Wozniak replied quickly, 'but I do enjoy sex.'

Bridget shook her head in silence, as if she couldn't believe what she had just heard.

'Did Julie often ask you to stay overnight?' Kingston said, taking charge again.

'No! She did not. Occasionally she went down to London to take in a show with girlfriends and stay overnight, but that's all. But this was different. She didn't say so openly, but I am sure she had met someone she thought was special.'

'But you have no idea who it might have been—'
'No!'
'Or where she might have met him?'
'No! Of course not. Or I would have told you, wouldn't I?'

Kingston held up his hand. 'Bridget, we are just trying to gather whatever information we can so that we can catch Julie's killer. So I do need to ask you if you think it could possibly be the case that she was going to meet her ex-husband.'

'God, no!'

'People do sometimes try to re-establish relationships that have broken down. Maybe he had contacted her.'

'If you knew what she told me about her husband, you would know that she would never have gone off to meet him with a broad smile across her face.' Bridget pursed her lips. 'Bob Tapper was a bastard,' she said, looking around as if she were afraid he might be hiding in one of the neighbours' front gardens, watching and listening from behind a bush. 'He controlled her. Hit her. She was scared of him. In the end she left him, but he wouldn't leave her alone.'

'You mean he stalked her?' Wozniak said. 'Did she report it?'

'Oh yes, she told you lot all about it, but a fat lot of good it did.'

'When was this?' Kingston said quickly.

'Three or four years ago.'

'And have you seen him at all recently?'

'I've not seen him since they split up. I only met him a couple of times. They lived in London and when she visited Marjorie, she mostly came alone.'

'Has Julie said anything about him trying to get in touch recently?'

'Not to me. Not to her mother either, or I would have heard about it.'

'Well, thank you,' Kingston said. 'You have been most helpful. We'll ring you later once we have made the arrangements for you and Mrs Baxter to come and make a formal identification of the body. Ideally that would be tomorrow, as it is a matter of some urgency.'

Bridget shivered and turned away, up to the front door and inside the house without a backward glance.

'So, what do you think?' Wozniak said as she belted herself into the car.

'Looking round at the photographs there, what I would say is that she was a very attractive woman, and that maybe she didn't always tell either of those two what she was up to. Innocent nights out with girlfriends, likewise trips to London, chances are men and sex were involved.'

Wozniak said nothing, preferring to keep her thoughts to herself. She was learning fast that Kingston liked to be in control.

CHAPTER 3

'Aaaaghhhh!' The scream ripped through the sterile air of the laboratory and through the long featureless corridor down which Bridget Moore had just pushed Marjorie Baxter. It might have been a poacher caught in a trap, or a man who had just received a kick in his testicles, but it came from Marjorie Baxter. It needed no skills of deduction to conclude that this meant the dead woman on the metal slab was indeed Baxter's daughter.

Kingston and Royce had been waiting in the corridor. Both men were taken unawares by this outburst, and stood rooted to the spot, uncertain how to proceed. So they were relieved when Bridget Moore took charge, pushed her friend back along the corridor and out into the car park, and drove away.

'Do they always react like that?' Royce said, displaying his inexperience and callowness.

Kingston grunted and puffed out his cheeks. 'At least we know who she is. Now we can push on and find the bastard.'

* * *

'I've been checking out Bob Tapper.'

Wozniak had approached Kingston rather nervously, not sure how he would react. He looked up and frowned. 'Who?'

'Bob Tapper, the ex-partner of Julie Baxter.'

'He's hardly a priority now.'

'With respect, sir, he has a bit of a history.'

'You mean as a serial killer?' Kingston sneered, and Wozniak sensed the others — especially Royce — looking up from their computers and listening in with fascination as the sergeant cut her down to size. An open-plan office was the perfect place to do it.

'For domestic violence and stalking.'

'Are you saying he was taken to court and found guilty?'

'No. But that doesn't mean—'

'What it means, Constable,' Kingston snapped, loud and aggressive, 'is that Bob Tapper sits at the bottom of our priority list and . . .' He paused, as a sudden thought crossed his mind. He smirked, liking the thought very much indeed. He glanced around, conscious of the undisguised interest of the others around him. 'What it means, Constable Wozniak, is that tracking down Bob Tapper will therefore be assigned to you to follow through on, because I cannot afford to waste the time of more experienced staff on it.'

'Yes, sir.'

'But only so long as it doesn't get in the way of any other tasks that have been assigned to you. Police work isn't glamorous. There's reporting, following up on the house-to-houses that haven't been done, dealing with the paperwork. Is that clear?'

She nodded.

'Is that clear, Constable?'

'Yes, sir.'

With that, she retreated back to her desk, all too conscious of the barely concealed amusement of several of the other staff.

* * *

Wozniak stayed in the station late that evening, trying to assemble the history and movements of Bob Tapper. The break-up between him and Julie Baxter had taken place some

three and a half years previously. They were both on the system — Julie had called the police twice while they were still
together — but on both occasions there had been no action
taken. *A domestic*, one officer had written, as if it didn't matter, as if violence between a man and his wife was something
that wasn't important enough for the police. On the third
occasion, Julie had complained that he was stalking her. She
must have made the break from him by then. She was living
at a different address, but still in the Ealing area. If she had
expected help then, she might as well have been . . . Wozniak
frowned, trying to recall the English expression — she was
always trying to improve her English. Whistling something
. . . yes, that was it, whistling in the wind.

She smiled to herself, and then felt guilty. There was
nothing to smile about. She had read about it on the inter-
net. Stalking protection orders had been introduced in 2020,
but what good had they done? She hadn't seen the figures
for London, but the Thames Valley Police had not applied
for a single one between January 2020 and January 2021.
Didn't stalking exist here? Anger surging through her, she
looked down and realized that her hands had turned into
fists. *Breathe*, she told herself, *open up your fingers, let your body
relax. In out, in out, in and out.*

She turned her focus back to the job in hand, to poor
Julie Baxter. Perhaps moving to Oxfordshire, well away from
London, had brought her a semblance of peace. At least there
hadn't been any incidents recently, or at least none had been
reported. And yet now she was dead. Had the bastard tracked
her down here and killed her when she rejected him again?
That was the obvious conclusion, and was what she wanted
to believe, but was there the evidence to prove it? That was
her job, and what Kingston and Holden wanted her to do.
Find the evidence.

There was the sudden noise of a door banging and heavy
footsteps approaching. It was well past 9 p.m. and the open-
plan office in which she was based had been empty of other

staff for nearly an hour. Another bang and the door was rammed open. It was Jim Royce.

'Well, well, well! Look at you. Working all hours in order to keep in the good books of Detective Inspector Susan.'

'Good evening, Jim,' she said.

He advanced towards her, almost stumbling over a chair as he did so. He reached her, placed his hands on her desk and leaned forward. He stank of alcohol. 'Fancy a drink, Krys?'

'Krystyna.'

'I prefer Krys. It's more friendly.'

'I'm going home in a minute.'

'I could give you a lift.'

'No, thank you.'

'Don't you like men then?'

'Some men are very nice.'

He stared at her for several seconds, and despite the fact that she was sitting in the safety of a police station, she felt the stirrings of fear. There would be others on duty downstairs, but up here there was just her and him — a man who had drunk too much, a man who thought he was *the* man, a man who . . .

Suddenly he pushed himself upright again. 'I reckon our Susan has her eye on you. You want to watch out or she'll have your knickers off quicker than you can say "Polski."' He laughed, wandered over to his desk where he scrabbled around in the drawers before stumbling off to the door and out of sight.

She sat there for two or three minutes, waiting to recover. Once, when a guy had groped her, she had kneed him in the groin — thank God she had just completed a self-defence class — and he had collapsed to the ground clutching himself, and she had been able to hail a taxi. But sitting at her desk, she had been taken unawares by Jim Royce. She had felt the fear of a woman being preyed on. When had Julie felt that fear? In the cinema or afterwards? Had Tapper been outside waiting for her, or had someone else? Maybe someone she knew from somewhere, who had had a couple of drinks and wanted something more to round off his evening? Had that private detective persuaded her to accept a lift home and then insisted on payback? Susan seemed certain that he wasn't the type, but could she really know? Maybe Julie had once been Mullen's client? She considered this. It seemed unlikely, but perhaps she should be checking that out too. Or maybe she had been the victim of one of his clients? Now that was a thought. Someone whose life he had messed up, and who knew too much about him. Surely, clients of private detectives must have plenty of nasty, embarrassing secrets that they would do anything to keep secret?

There was another noise, another set of footsteps approaching. She tensed, poised to get to her feet if it was Royce again, but it was Susan Holden who pushed open the door. She seemed oblivious to Wozniak's presence, but then stopped suddenly halfway to her cubicle. 'Go home,' she said tersely. 'Get some food and some rest.'

'Just finishing something off,' Wozniak replied.

'That's an order. I want you to be useful tomorrow, and that means alert and not half asleep.'

'Yes, ma'am.'

CHAPTER 4

Mullen was feeling guilty. Living with Becca was exhausting, and the last few weeks had been hell. She had taken him in when he had nowhere else to go. She had put up with being kidnapped and damn near murdered. She had even put up with Rex, his dog.

He ought to have been grateful, and in many ways he was. He had become fond of her, so fond that at times he had thought she might allow him to migrate upstairs from the sofa bed on which he was sleeping to the welcoming warmth of her double bed. But Becca had her own history, including a pregnancy about which she refused to talk. Mullen would have considered it an honour, a supreme act of friendship, if she had just confided in him. He would have forgiven her anything then. Not that there was, as far as he was concerned, anything to forgive. But Becca had never dropped her defences.

Things are never the same after you have given birth. That was what people — mothers mostly — often said. But Becca's baby had been still-born, so for her that trite saying — which should have referred to endless breastfeeding, sleep-deprived nights, croup, nappies and the constant washing of tiny clothes — was true in another, tragic sense. Nothing would ever be the same. What she would have given for a baby that woke her every two hours for a feed, for the smell of filled nappies and the exhaustion motherhood involves.

Mullen had been three hours' drive away when it happened, and to this day felt he was being punished for it, even though he was not the father. He had failed her in her hour of greatest need. Not that she had ever blamed him, but he would have understood it if she had. He would have gladly listened to her and embraced her agony, but she never spoke about it at all. The baby — Becca had named her Alice — was a no-go area.

He felt guilty now because he was leaving her on her own again. Only for an hour or two, only to meet up with a potential client, just a case of popping out really — but he felt mighty guilty all the same. He also felt mightily relieved that he had a genuine excuse to escape the house. The depression that had descended on Becca seemed to have permeated the place and everything in it. Even the dog seemed to have been infected. Which was another reason why Mullen had brought him along. Rex, he decided, could do with a change of scene too.

They were going to meet a new client — or rather a potential new client. Mullen had been disappointed too many times to count his chickens before an upfront payment had entered his bank account. People often assumed he would work for next to nothing if they chatted him up enough, or that he would work on a no-win no-fee basis. He wasn't a lawyer working on cast-iron cases. He was a man struggling like everyone else to make a living in a dog-eat-dog world. He glanced down as if the dog could read his thoughts. 'Sorry, Rex.' He often spoke to Rex. 'It's just a manner of speech. I know dogs rarely eat dogs.'

Rex gave him a look that warned Mullen to concentrate on his driving. Then he settled down again, and within seconds he was whimpering softly, dreaming (perhaps) of chasing rabbits and (for the first time in his life) catching one. Mullen shook his head and did as his dog had told him.

The rendezvous point was in the middle of Oxford. Not much chance of Rex finding a rabbit there, but Mullen had set out early. Traffic permitting — a big ask in Oxford — he would have plenty of time to let the dog have a good run in the University Parks before heading to the Turf Tavern. Mullen had only been there once. Paying a visit to Oxford's most famous and popular pub had seemed an essential part of getting to know the city. Tucked away out of sight, it had been heaving with students, tourists and businesspeople in suits reliving their youths. But quite why someone wanting to hire a private detective would choose to meet in such an indiscreet place was puzzling.

By the time he had parked in St Giles', toured the University Parks and bagged up two of Rex's turds, he had ten minutes to spare. Being a man who prided himself on never being late (*army habits are hard to shake off* should have been tattooed on his chest), he felt unusually content. Everything had gone to plan. What could possibly go wrong?

As if in response to Mullen's hubristic thoughts, it began to rain, not just a light drizzle that could be ignored, but a deluge that sent unsuspecting pedestrians scurrying for cover. Mullen zipped up his jacket, ducked his head and increased his pace, heading south down Parks Road. Rex whined in complaint. He wasn't so dumb as to suppose Mullen was heading back to the shelter of the car.

As he approached the junction with Broad Street, Mullen hesitated. There were two ways into the Turf Tavern, both narrow passages, one from Holywell Street and one from New College Lane. The former was closest, but he pressed straight across the road, because he had spotted his quarry — or at least he thought he had, a striking figure in a long green coat and red boots. It had to be her. She had turned onto Catte Street from the Broad and marched diagonally across the road. A delivery lorry stopped sharply in front of her. The driver flashed his lights but the woman seemed oblivious. Moments later, she had disappeared round the corner. Mullen grabbed the dog, tucked him under his arm and accelerated across the road. When he reached the corner of Catte Street, he spotted her again. Kat ("with a 'K,'" she had insisted over the phone) had passed under the Bridge of Sighs, but now she hesitated. She was looking around. Mullen raised a hand but she showed no sign of spotting or recognizing him. Instead, she plunged forward again, into St Helen's Passage and out of view. Mullen strode on but slowed his pace. He had no desire to alarm her by shouting out her name — she had sounded anxious over the phone. He would approach her calmly in the pub.

The Turf was sprinkled with the usual suspects — students and tourists — as well as a sizeable group of besuited office workers. Mullen slipped past the people queuing at the bar and then, to his surprise, saw that she had already established herself at a small table in the corner. He made his way across to her. 'I'm Doug. You must be Kat.'

'With a "K."' She looked at him with disconcertingly blue eyes and a blank face. 'I haven't got my handbag with me. Would you mind getting me a gin and tonic?'

'Of course.'

Of course? What sort of mug was he? She had summoned him to a meeting. She ought to be paying. But Mullen was all too often a soft touch where women were concerned, even women significantly older than himself.

'You can leave your dog with me,' she said. 'I'm perfectly safe.'

'So kind,' she murmured when Mullen returned. Rex was sitting up on her lap, looking around, king of all he surveyed. Mullen sat down and watched in astonishment as Kat drained her drink with barely a ripple of her throat. 'Don't they approve?' she said.

Mullen sipped at his orange juice. 'They?'

'Are you a Muslim, Mr Mullen?'

'No.'

'You have taken the pledge then?'

'No. I'll maybe have a beer at home this evening.'

But she seemed to have lost interest, because she was looking around the pub, frowning. 'I used to come here as an undergraduate. The drink was much cheaper in the junior common room, of course, but sometimes you just needed to get away from college. To meet men. We all wanted to do that!' She giggled, and her eyes assumed a faraway, quizzical look. Where was she? Back in her student days? Had it changed much since then? The style of dress no doubt, and most certainly it would have been full of smoke. Or had the nicotine addicts been driven outside by then? Mullen sipped at his juice and waited in vain for her to return to the present moment.

'Kat,' he said firmly, 'did you want my help with something?'

A puzzled frown.

'When people ask to meet me,' he continued, 'it is almost always because they want me to help them in some way.'

She leaned forward conspiratorially. Mullen paused, then did the same. She was wearing a scent that hinted at violets and sweet peas. 'Mr Mullen, I feel things.'

Mullen tried not to let his own feelings show, but he failed miserably. Her face collapsed and she leaned back against her seat. 'I can see you don't believe me.'

He looked down in embarrassment. She was a nice old woman, lost in her university days and maybe a bit doolally. He could surely have done a more convincing job of taking her seriously. He tried again. 'What sort of things do you feel?'

'What is your dog called?'

'Rex.'

Rex was still sitting on her lap. She began to slowly run her hands down either side of his body. Not quite stroking, more like probing. Her eyes were half closed, her head tilted to one side. After a minute of this, she looked up at Mullen. 'He misses his mother.'

'His mother?'

'His human mother. She looked after him very well. What was her name?'

Mullen told her.

'It must have been traumatic for him.'

'What do you mean?'

'You know what I mean.' She bent down until her face was touching the dog's hair. 'I can still smell the fire.'

Mullen felt his throat tighten. Images of flames and his desperate attempt to enter the house flashed across his brain. Even the smell of the black smoke, acrid and choking, which had emanated from the scorched double-glazed units. And the sound of Rex yapping frenziedly in the background.

'You . . . how do you know?'

She raised a hand, as if answering were too much for her. Suddenly, she looked exhausted.

'Are you all right?'

Another wave of the hand. 'Please, a coffee,' she whispered. 'If you don't mind, Mr Mullen.'

Mullen fought his way to the bar. As he queued, he looked back. Rex was still sitting on her lap, alert, doing his *Monarch of the Glen* impression. She was biting into a banana while frowning at her mobile phone. He ordered the drinks, remembering this time to ask for the receipt so he could claim them as expenses, and wondering at the same time if she was genuine. She was certainly strange. Eventually, he got his drinks and began to edge his way back through the scrum, balancing the two coffees, the milk and sugar on a small round beer tray. It wasn't until he reached the table and looked up that he realized she was no longer there.

'Where is she?' he said, but Rex, who was sitting on her seat, didn't let on.

The ladies, he assumed. Mullen settled down and began to sip at his coffee. Eventually he got up, made his way to the toilets and asked a young woman to, please, see if there was someone called Kat in there. 'I'm worried she might have been taken ill.' But Kat wasn't there. He tried ringing her mobile, but it went straight to the answering service. He returned to the table. Rex was now lying down, spread out on the bench seat, and looked happy to remain there. But Mullen had had enough. He pulled on his damp coat. 'Come on,' he said.

The dog whined.

Mullen leaned down to scoop him up and saw he had been lying on something: under his front paws was a thin paperback. Mullen stuffed it in his pocket. This was neither the time nor the place to check out Kat's taste in literature. When he saw her again — or rather if — he would give it back to her unsullied.

* * *

When he got home, Mullen tried ringing and texting Kat again, but failed to make contact. For the rest of that day she bobbed around on the surface of his thoughts. Who was she? Why had she arranged to meet him? And why ask him to buy her a coffee and then do a disappearing act? By the next morning, he had given a metaphorical shrug of the shoulders. Water under the bridge. Maybe she had just got cold feet at the last minute, or maybe she had a mental health issue. *I feel things.* What was that all about? In any case, he had more pressing matters to deal with, namely a job that paid a very tidy daily rate and for which he had received £800 upfront. So, he forgot about her — almost — and over the next few days focused his attention on the job in hand. Dull days of watching, tailing, hanging around and generally getting bored.

On the Saturday morning, the job completed, he allowed himself a lie in. He was sleeping on the sofa bed downstairs in the large room that acted as kitchen, dining room and TV lounge. Becca was still on sick leave and she was not an early riser. It was Rex who woke him, desperate for a pee. He let the dog out for a pee and then clambered back under his duvet, only to hear Becca's heavy tread on the stairs.

'Not working today, Doug?'

He sat up and was surprised to see that she was fully dressed. She was wearing one of three maternity dresses she had purchased early in her pregnancy — the purple one.

'No.'

'I see.' *I see.* These words can have multiple meanings and none, but expressed in the way Becca had just done, they were all extremely negative. He suspected she just wanted her house back. Maybe he had outstayed his welcome. 'We can have breakfast together,' he suggested as he eased himself to his feet. 'Do a crossword.'

Becca sniffed ostentatiously. 'Maybe you should take a shower.'

Mullen felt a snarl of anger rise through his chest. He was pretty good at personal hygiene. And he really had done his utmost to humour her and support her through the last weeks and months, putting up with her lying in bed half the day feeling sorry for herself, never getting around to cleaning or clearing up anything, and here she was making sarcastic remarks about him.

An hour later, after a breakfast eaten in a silence interrupted occasionally by almost monosyllabic exchanges, Becca pulled on her oversized coat and departed the house without as much as a "Goodbye," banging the door as she went. As he finished the washing up and wiped down the surfaces, Doug watched her making her way down the lane before turning left onto the public footpath across the fields. He remained standing there for some time after he was done, still staring out of the windows, lost in thoughts and regrets.

Eventually he made his way upstairs. He told himself that this was so he could brush his teeth, but when he got to the small landing he stopped. There were three doors. To the right was Becca's bedroom, to the left the bathroom, and in front of him was the door that opened into the spare bedroom. Or rather it might have been the spare bedroom, but ever since Becca had taken him in, it had always been the baby's room. He had been banned from it. He continued to hesitate. He hadn't been into it since before the disaster. He took a couple of deep breaths. Becca was out, so this was an opportunity. It was bound to be dusty in there, he told himself. He could give it a quick wipe over and a vacuum. Maybe it could do with an airing. The excuses advanced across the parade ground of his mind and were now standing smartly to attention in front of him, asking him if that wasn't the one thing he could do for Becca: go in and give the baby's room a quick clean. She'd probably not notice, and if she did, she'd be privately grateful.

He opened the door before he could change his mind, stepped inside and looked around. He had painted it for her, even though the baby was nothing to do with him. After all, she had taken him in when he had been homeless with nowhere else to go, so decorating the room had been the least he could do for her. She had known the baby was going to be a girl, but she had refused to let Mullen in on the secret and had insisted that the room be painted half blue and half pink.

'No stereotyping, Mullen.'

'Shouldn't you clear this with the letting agents?' he had said.

She had laughed. 'No way!'

This could have been the last time he had heard her laugh. She certainly hadn't since the birth of her baby, Alice. Poor little Alice had been born dead, after a traumatic labour, and by the time Mullen had driven three hours back from a bit of personal business, it was all over. He had arrived to find Becca lying exhausted and distraught in the hospital bed, clutching what should have been her bundle of joy, and had known the worst. Poor little Alice. And poor Becca, who had lain there, silent and unresponsive. She had let Alice slip out of her arms and Mullen himself had picked her up, keeping watch over her until a nurse gently took her away from him. It was Mullen who wept.

Now, as he stood in the doorway of the little bedroom, the horror of that day returned. He felt a deep shame at his earlier irritation and self-pitying anger. What did any of it matter when compared with the trauma that she was still living with, day and night? She had tried to go back to work a couple of weeks after the disaster, but had crashed and burned less than a month later. *You should have got over it by now*, he had sometimes felt like saying to her, knowing it was the last thing he should ever say. Why should she have "got over it?" Was there a time limit to these things?

Mullen wiped at his cheek with the back of his wrist. He wiped again, but the tears kept on coming. Becca had not cried in the hospital and she had not cried since coming home — or at least not in front of him. Now, with her out walking, it was his opportunity to give himself up to her grief. *Snap out of it. Suppose she comes back?* Mullen looked around the room again, his gaze only coming to a stop when it reached the small children's wardrobe. He stood there, mesmerized. He moved forward, placed his hand on the little Winnie the Pooh knob and pulled the flimsy door open. Inside there was a pack of disposable nappies on one side and a pile of baby clothes on the other — blue and pink Babygros, tiny white vests and various matinee jackets knitted by her friends and colleagues. On top of the pile was a single striped hat. He reached out and touched it, barely able to breathe. It was a terrible reminder of what might have been and what could not be forgotten. He was not a religious man, but he muttered some words that he hoped would pass for a prayer. Then he backed out of the room and closed the door softly on the memories within.

Mullen was sitting at the table, checking his emails, when Becca returned. She pushed open the door and looked around, puffing and wheezing, her face red.

'Where's my phone?'

'On the windowsill.' Mullen pointed. 'Everything all right?'

'No, it isn't.'

'So what's up?'

But she wasn't listening. She grabbed the phone and was soon telling someone on the end of the line that she needed the ambulance service and the police. 'I've found the body of a woman and she's dead . . . yes, she's very, very dead . . . Yes of course I can tell when someone is dead. I'm an Accident and Emergency nurse.'

* * *

When a police car and an ambulance swept down the lane, Becca and Mullen were waiting outside the front door. The emergency service vehicles could be said to be travelling in convoy, except that to Mullen's jaundiced eye, they were more like rivals than allies. Each seemed eager to be first to the body — the paramedics with their stretcher and bags of tricks, the two uniformed officers in stab vests and their own equipment, as if expecting (and hoping for) the worst.

'Follow me!' Becca instructed, and marched off away from the house. She had discarded her coat and was resplend-ent in purple. They followed eagerly but meekly, as if recog-nizing that they had encountered a superior life force. Mullen locked the dog inside the house (poor Rex would definitely be an unwelcome complication) and followed at a slight dis-tance, wondering at the transformation in Becca — how in the presence of this death she had suddenly become so alive. She strode along like the Pied Piper of Hamelin, leading her followers along the side of a field of kale (whether intended as feed for animals or humans, Mullen wasn't sure), across the middle of a field of winter wheat (the farmer had told him what it was only a week or so previously), then along a rutted farm track to an old barn. Mullen had sheltered there a couple of times, to escape a sudden onslaught of rain, but as he approached this time he felt a mixture of anxiety and excitement quickening his pulse.

'Wait there!'

The shorter of the two female officers held up her hand as if she had missed her vocation as a 1960s traffic control copper. 'We don't want either of you compromising the crime scene.'

'Is it a crime scene?' Mullen said.

'A potential crime scene.' She gave him a hard stare. *Pedantic dickhead!* Mullen was good at interpreting such things.

While the paramedics attended to the body, the police produced blue-and-white tape and started to rig up a cordon. Mullen, who had caught up with Becca now, stood next to her and gasped. The paramedic who had been kneeling down on the near side of the body stood up.

'Shit!' Mullen said out loud.

'What?' Becca replied.

'The coat. It's green.'

'Very observant, Doug.'

'And she's wearing red boots.'

'What's your point, Doug?'

'I think it's the woman I met the other day. At the Turf in Oxford. The one who disappeared.'

'Excuse me, sir.' The two police officers had temporarily lost interest in their cordon and instead had turned to face Mullen, eyeing him up with considerable and unnerving interest. 'Are we to understand,' the tall one said, 'that you know the deceased, sir?'

'Yes, I believe I do.'

* * *

It felt like *déjà vu* — two detectives sitting opposite him across a tasteless utility table. One was DS Andy Kingston along with his rugby-battered square face, florid complexion and hard-man persona that he probably practised every morning in front of the mirror. The other was not DC Royce. Mullen wondered why that was. His replacement was a DC Krystyna Wozniak. She had blonde hair (dyed, Mullen reckoned), a delicate bone structure, a Polish accent and a tight mouth that looked like it never smiled. He wondered if they were going to do the good-cop, bad-cop routine. Wozniak brought him a mug of tea, for which he was grateful, though when he took a sip, he winced. She had put several spoons of sugar in it. Maybe that was her way of demonstrating she could be as hard as Kingston. Mullen tried not to care.

'I'd like to go over a few of the details again,' Kingston said.

Again. The word reverberated like the toll of doom. He had already given a statement to the uniformed police, but now here he was at the Cowley station on a Saturday night, being questioned by a couple of detectives who ought to have been either out having fun or at home slumped in front of *Match of the Day*.

'Couldn't this have waited until Monday?' Mullen said. Hadn't they got bigger fish to fry than him?

'Humour me,' said the humourless Kingston.

Mullen's solicitor patted Mullen on the back of his wrist, a warning to not get too smart. She cleared her throat and tapped her pen on the surface of the table. Althea Potter was grey-haired and middle-aged, and looked a soft touch. Appearances can be deceptive. 'My client has already provided a statement, and he feels strongly that dragging him here at this time of night was unnecessary. We do hope you have good reason for so doing? If not, others might view your actions as — how shall I put it? — egregiously oppressive.'

Mullen wasn't sure what she meant by *egregiously*, but he liked the tone of what she was saying.

Kingston smiled insincerely. 'Now that we have gathered more information, we just want to clarify some of the details of your client's statement, just in case there was any misunderstanding.'

Misunderstanding? Mullen didn't like the implications behind that word — not one little bit. Nor did he care for the look in Kingston's eyes, which were shining in anticipation, like a fox that has scented a lone chicken. Mullen was beginning to feel distinctly uneasy, but he was determined not to show it. 'Fire away,' he said.

Kingston nodded. 'The woman you met at the pub, whom you call Kat, are you sure you didn't know her?'

Mullen sighed, not because he was trying to make a theatrical point, but because he was tired and he didn't want to be there. 'It was the first time I have ever seen her. She rang up the night before. It will show up on my mobile phone records. I expect you've already looked at them, but if not, be my guest. And yes, she called herself Kat, with a "K."'

'Called herself?'

'My clients rarely give their real names at first. Maybe she is a Kat. Maybe she isn't. Didn't she have some form of ID on her?'

'Why did she want to hire you?'

'She didn't say.'

'Didn't you ask?'

'It's not a thing you ask over the phone.'

'Why did you arrange to meet at the Turf?'

'It was her suggestion.' He paused. 'Maybe she liked the beer there.'

Potter made a noise of disapproval. *Cut the flippancy*, the noise said.

Kingston pressed steadily on, sensing that he was making progress. 'And how were you going to identify her?'

'She said she would be wearing a green coat and red boots.'

'So you met up with her in the Turf and—'

'And I bought us both a drink, and she started to tell me how she felt things.'

'Felt things?'

'That's what she said: "I feel things."'

'And what did you think she meant by that?'

'I wasn't quite sure at first.'

'You didn't think she was unhinged?'

'I try not to make snap judgements of people. She seemed perfectly pleasant. Maybe a bit eccentric, but that's not a crime in my book.'

'Tell me about your dog,' Kingston said in a sudden change of direction.

'His name is Rex. He's a Westiepoodle. He's fully up to date with his vaccinations and—'

Althea Potter sucked in noisily through her teeth, silencing Mullen.

Kingston glanced at his colleague and gave her what Mullen assumed to be a meaningful look. Wozniak nodded and took over the baton. 'Mr Mullen. We are both puzzled as to why you should take a dog to a meeting with a client in a pub.'

'He rides shotgun with me.' Tiredness makes people behave in various ways, including being inappropriately flippant. Mullen could feel Potter tensing.

'You think I am stupid, Mr Mullen?' Wozniak started at him, her eyes curiously blank, showing no sign of the anger that she might reasonably be feeling. 'You think I do not know what that expression means?'

'No.'

'You think you will try and trick this Polish copper with your smart English?'

Mullen said nothing, but he felt suddenly embarrassed, and indeed ashamed of himself. He looked down, unable to look her in the eye.

'You see, Mr Mullen, you are using the dog as your trump card. You understand trump card? Or do I need to explain my meaning?'

'I understand the expression. But I don't understand why you think me taking my dog to a pub is a trump card.'

'Because you spin us a story about the woman sitting Rex on her knee and then pretending she can tell you things about yourself, because that will explain how your dog's hairs have got onto her coat.'

'I often take the dog with me. But if I had been planning to kill the poor woman, I think I would have had the sense to leave Rex at home.'

Wozniak uttered a guttural sound which indicated she wasn't impressed. 'Mr Mullen, I think you are a little frightened. You think I am sitting here trying to catch you out so that we can lock you up and throw away the key. Yes?'

He nodded.

'Right now, I am trying to find out everything I can about this woman, Kat. Because I want to get to the truth, whatever that is. So I will ask you this, and I hope you will think hard before you answer. Is there anything else that she said or did that you have not told me, however trivial you might think it to be?'

Mullen leaned back as far as his chair allowed and urged his mind to range over that short and fateful meeting — the rain, the drink she swallowed without pausing, her "feeing things" and smelling the dog, the coffee he paid for and carried to the table to discover she had done a runner. His brain stopped and rewound. 'Only one thing,' he said. 'When I went to buy us both a coffee, I looked back and she was eating a banana.'

'A banana?'

'Yes. Is that trivial enough for you?'

Potter gave a rat-a-tat on the table with her pen. Kingston uttered the noise of a rat being strangled. But Wozniak remained utterly silent, and her eyes remained fixed on Mullen, compelling him to return her stare.

'Thank you, Mr Mullen. I can see you are very tired, but I do have just one more question. How old did you estimate this woman — this Kat — to be?'

Mullen frowned. In the circumstances, since they had the body, it seemed a rather superfluous question. 'I would estimate somewhere between sixty and sixty-five.'

Wozniak turned and looked at Kingston, and he looked back at her. A pair of meaningful looks. Mullen felt a shiver of unease ripple through his body.

'Detective Sergeant Kingston, Detective Constable Wozniak, what are you not telling us?' Potter snapped. 'I shall instruct my client to make no further comment until we know.'

* * *

When Mullen got back to the cottage, he was surprised to find Becca still up, watching a late-night movie on the TV. He wasn't at all sure how she would react. She had been so not herself these last months that judging how she would react to any situation had become impossible. Mostly she showed a silent indifference, and so far she had displayed no interest in the woman he had chatted to in the cinema. Or rather a cold indifference to whatever it was that he and she had said or done together.

She had briefly shown her temper when the police had come the other morning, but otherwise she had studiously avoided asking him about it. When he had tried to talk about it, she had tossed a caustic "your love life is nothing to do with me" at him, but that had been it.

So when she jumped up from her chair and threw her arms around him, Mullen was taken by surprise. 'I was worried about you,' she confessed. 'I thought maybe you were going to be locked up for the night.'

He wrapped his arms around her too, enjoying the feeling, but without warning, she detached herself. 'I expect you could do with a drink,' she said.

'Yes.'

'So could I.'

When they both had a gin and tonic in front of them, she tersely asked him what had happened. But while he talked, she remained as silent as a monolith — and as unresponsive. At the end, he drained the rest of his drink and went to the sink, where he rinsed and dried it. Then he turned and looked at her. She was still, so still she could have been a waxwork at Madame Tussauds. She had barely touched her gin.

'Doug,' she said. Her voice was razor sharp.

'Yes?'

She sat there unmoving, looking at her glass as if it were a crystal ball. He waited, desperate for her to say something, to show an interest in him, to demonstrate that she cared. That sudden hug had seemed so important and yet she had cut if off with brutal suddenness.

47

'I think you've been in Alice's room.'

Mullen froze, a schoolboy caught in the act, unable to look at the teacher.

'In fact, I know you have. I stuck a hair across the door. Like James Bond in one of the 007 films. It's very effective.'

'It must be.'

'So why did you?'

'I felt I needed to. It was this morning, while you were out. I'm sorry. I know you told me not to and I—'

She lunged forward and grabbed his wrist, her long nails digging in so sharply that he let out an involuntary yelp. But he didn't pull away, accepting the pain. Maybe he deserved it.

'You think I should clear it all out, let you sleep in there instead of on the sofa bed?'

'No.'

'So why did you go and snoop around in there?' she demanded. 'Why did you *need* to?'

'Because . . .' The words were on the tip of his tongue, and yet . . . it was like drawing attention to the elephant in the room, a risky thing at the best of times. But there was no alternative. He looked across at her, seeing the fury in her eyes — and something else too. Elemental grief, he thought. 'This may sound a bit mad,' he said, 'but I needed to remind myself of the trauma you went through and the pain you must still be feeling, and . . .' He trailed to a halt. There was a lump of grief stuck in his throat. What else could he say? 'Because I care for you, Becca.'

'You care for me, do you? Like you care for your little dog.'

Her words sliced across the room like shards of glass. Mullen reeled under the pain. He had once been slashed across the face with a cutthroat razor, and this felt worse.

'You know it's much more than that.'

'Do I?'

'I would do anything for you,' he said quietly.

'You mean like commit murder?' she said, and her eyes bored into him. She wasn't joking.

Mullen gasped. Even in her volatile state, this was beyond comprehension. This wasn't her. This was like an alien being that had invaded her body.

'What the hell have you been up to, Doug?'

'Nothing.'

'Apart from chatting up women in cinemas and pubs, women who then end up dead.'

'Hey, that's not fair. I talked to a woman in the cinema. I was a bit worried about her. As for the pub, she was a client, or so I thought. An old woman—'

'You claim she was old. Why the hell should I believe you? The dead body tells a very different story.'

Mullen ran his hands through his hair, tugging at it in distress. 'You can't think I'm a—'

'I'm going to bed, Doug, and you can bloody well stay downstairs tonight. If you need to have a piss, do it in the garden — like your wretched dog. Just stay out of my bathroom.'

CHAPTER 5

When you weigh up all the pros and cons, death will be a kindness. What does life hold for her now? I didn't plan it this way from the start. It just . . . evolved. I would have been quite happy for her to go into a gentle decline and then one day she would slip away and I would inherit without any complications.

As for Ngung, she only has herself to blame. If that stupid Vietnamese bitch hadn't got pregnant, none of this would have happened. I kept her supplied with the pill, because I didn't want the hassle of wearing a condom — it takes away all the fun and the spontaneity. She must have stopped taking them. Maybe she never did take them, just pretended to. Maybe she wanted to get pregnant, to have my baby, so she could use it to manipulate me and force me to look after her for ever, and to give her family more money.

She didn't tell me. She tried to keep it a secret, but one morning, passing her bathroom — she had her own bathroom, you see I treated her well — I smelled the sickly odour of vomit and I put two and two together. Did she really think I wouldn't notice?

I told her very calmly that I would organize a termination — private, quiet, safe. But she went into a screaming fit, and she only stopped when I gave her a good slap.

That shut her up, but later, when I thought about it, I realized something else. She couldn't be trusted. How could I be sure that she wouldn't say something to someone else, someone who came to the door? And what about when her pregnancy became obvious? What then?

Because, of course, people do come to the door. Julie the hairdresser for example. Hairdressers like to talk, of course, and ask questions, and she would have been one of the first to notice. Maybe she already had.

So I made a point of being around at her next appointment, so that I could monitor things. Sometimes I am able to work from home, but in those circumstances I usually remain in my office and summon Ngung when I need a coffee or something to eat. But this time I wandered through to the huge kitchen where the hairdressing always took place. I asked Julie how she was and even made all three of them a cup of tea. Julie was chatty, even flirtatious, and when she had finished with Kat, she offered to give me a trim.

'On the house!' she had giggled. And I agreed. It gave me an excuse to stay there and monitor things, so I told Ngung she could have a half-hour break. I wanted Julie to be relaxed, off her guard. I wanted to weigh her up.

I like having my hair cut by a woman. I enjoy the feeling of an attractive woman's body close to mine. She smelled nice too, a cheap perfume admittedly, but it helped. Sometimes her hands seemed to hover over my skin, sometimes they gently stroked the nape of my neck as she brushed aside loose hair.

I could see Kat watching from her chair, observing us over her mug of tea. Did she sense what was going on, that something wasn't quite right? Or was she away in her own world? I wasn't sure at the time, still am not. All I know is that I got rather excited, and yet there was nothing I could do then, no way I could do what I wanted to do.

'Thank you, Julie,' I said as she got out her mirror and showed me what she had done. 'You've got magic hands.'

She giggled again. 'My pleasure,' she whispered. 'But next time — if you'd like there to be a next time — I would like to make it clear that it won't be free.'

* * *

'Ma'am?'

Holden looked up to see Wozniak in the doorway. She didn't reply, her irritation at being disturbed radiating from every pore.

'Sorry, ma'am. It's just that I've taken a call from the pathologist, Frank Dickens, about the woman in the green coat. He wonders if someone would like to pop over? Andy and Jim are out on some other job, and I wasn't sure if I should go on my own or wait—'

'Don't wait. It might be important.' Holden was suddenly on full alert. She had a pile of virtual paperwork on her computer that she had been ploughing through. To describe this as boring didn't begin to do justice to it. Tedium beyond belief. Mind-numbing. Hell on earth. Whereas this was an opportunity to escape. Her born-again mother would have called it "an answer to prayer". Wozniak continued to hover in the doorway. The fact was she was inexperienced, and the case was definitely a rather unusual one. Holden reckoned she could reasonably argue that in the circumstances it would be a good way of observing her detective constable's ways of working. She stood up. 'I'll come with you. As Mr Mullen might say, I'll ride shotgun.'

Wozniak certainly drove well. Smooth, without fuss and without the emotionless tones of a satnav or the overexcited tones of a radio presenter in the background. Nor did she strike up a cascade of cheerful chatter. 'I had a bad night,' Holden said as soon as she got into the car, and Wozniak took the cue. Holden shut her eyes, letting her mind drift — Mullen, Baines, and two women apparently wearing the same green coat. Curiouser and curiouser, she mused, as her brain disappeared down the rabbit hole. Not to mention the added curiosity of Mullen possibly being the last person — except for the killer — to talk to Julie Baxter. Was that really coincidence?

The pathologist was a man that Holden had never encountered before. 'Frank Dickens,' he said, waving a greeting. 'No relation to Charles, if you're wondering. Or even if you're not.'

Holden didn't laugh. She introduced herself. 'You will address your comments and questions to my colleague, Detective Constable Krystyna Wozniak. I am here in the capacity of observer.'

Dickens nodded. 'Well, Krystyna, the cause of death was, as you may have surmised, an overdose of drugs. There is a single, very clear puncture wound in the lower right arm.'

'Administered by the victim herself?'

'Possibly.' Dickens scratched his head. 'It was a very significant overdose. And there are no signs that the poor girl—'

'Woman,' snapped Holden. 'She was a woman.'

Dickens froze for a moment or two before carrying on. 'Indeed. Just a manner of speech. There are no signs that the poor woman had previously taken drugs via injection. Her nostrils suggest she might have occasionally taken them recreationally, but that is all. However, on this occasion, she or someone else injected her with a very substantial dose, which would have rendered her unconscious very swiftly.'

'Is there any sign that this was administered against her will?' Wozniak said, taking back the reins.

'Nothing conclusive, I think.'

'But something not conclusive, maybe?' Wozniak's approach was softer, but otherwise not so different from Holden's own.

'There is some bruising on the woman's right wrist, quite recent I would say. But also some signs of older bruising.'

'And what, in your professional opinion, might this bruising on the wrist signify?' Wozniak asked.

Dickens considered his response for a few seconds. 'I can't give a precise answer, but it is consistent with her being gripped very tightly.'

'And the older bruising?'

Dickens shrugged. 'It looks as though she has been hit on at least a couple of occasions.'

'And how long before her death did she last eat?'

'Ah, that is an interesting question. Not for a considerable period of time. We have calculated her time of death at between four and seven a.m., but I would estimate that she hadn't eaten since lunchtime the previous day.'

Wozniak frowned, and then glanced at Holden, who took this as an opportunity to join in.

'I understand from one of my officers that you think the victim died where she was found.'

'Not think,' he replied waspishly. 'I can state that as a matter of fact.'

'A slip of the tongue,' she snapped back. The word sorry was not in Holden's vocabulary. All she did was glance across at Wozniak and nod almost imperceptibly.

'You have been most helpful,' Wozniak said with a generous smile. 'Is there anything else you can tell us now?'

Dickens smiled back. Holden felt jealousy flicker through her. The man had been seduced by Wozniak's charm and youthful beauty. 'Not at present,' he said, 'but I will let you know if anything else occurs to me.'

'Thank you.' Wozniak issued another siren smile. 'We do of course look forward to receiving your full report at the earliest possible opportunity.'

'Before we go . . .' Holden said quickly. 'I wonder if I could ask you to cast your mind back to Julie Baxter.'

'I think I sent a full report through to Andy Kingston.'

'Indeed you did, Frank. It was a model of thoroughness.' She tried to smile at him as Wozniak had but could tell it in no way had the same effect on him. 'I understand you are very experienced, and I wondered if Krystyna and myself could benefit from that experience.'

He nodded cautiously. Holden's reputation had gone before her.

'So, some of my officers have wondered if these two murders, committed within a few days of each other, might not have been committed by the same person. And we were wondering if perhaps you had discovered anything in your examinations that would point in that direction?'

Frank Dickens paused. It was as plain as a pikestaff that she was flattering him, and what man does not like to be flattered? He was no exception, and of course if the notoriously irascible Susan Holden was asking him for his professional help so obsequiously, then who was he to refuse her?

'I deal in facts, Susan,' he said. If she was calling him by his first name, he would respond in kind. 'Most obviously, both women were displaying signs of previous injuries, the sort of injuries that suggest domestic violence. Of course, you will know that this is by no means an uncommon experience for women in relationships with men, but whether it is significant in this case is a matter for you to determine.'

'What about forensics and prints?'

'Too soon for our second victim, but—'

'What about the coat?'

'In good time, Inspector,' he said, irritation in his voice.

'It's important, so please prioritize it.'

He stiffened. 'We will do our best.'

'Is there anything else you can tell us about our woman in the green coat?'

'A few fibres, that sort of thing, but that's about it. If you can find the killer, and he used his own car to transport her to where the body was found, then we might be able to cross-match the interior of the car and her clothing, but of course that wouldn't prove anything on its own. Maybe we will get lucky and will find skin under her nails, but there is no obvious sign of a struggle.'

'So you think she was drugged first, then driven to where the body was dumped.'

'I don't make such leaps of the imagination,' he said, again casting his smile towards Wozniak. 'I leave that to you police officers.'

Holden took in a deep breath. She had taken a distinct disliking to him, not least because of his pompous manner, but she knew that letting loose her irritation would be counterproductive. Even so, controlling her emotions in an anger management class was one thing, doing it in a real-life situation was much harder.

'Thank you so much,' Holden said, with icy politeness. 'You have been most enlightening.'

* * *

Kingston knocked on McPherson's door and barely paused before walking in. The detective superintendent looked up. 'Andy! How can I help you? Is everything going OK?'

'Yes and no.'

McPherson waved him to a chair. 'You've got five minutes.'

'I've got a problem with Detective Inspector Holden.'

'You're not the first.'

'She's very protective of Doug Mullen.'

'With good reason.'

'She said she would be staying clear of the case and letting me get on with it, and yet that isn't what's happening.'

'She's an experienced officer.' McPherson knew the course he was required to paddle, even though he had a lot of sympathy with the sergeant.

'Only this morning, she went round to Frank Dickens to receive his report on the second victim. Took Krystyna with her to cover herself. "Observing and training," she called it. Bloody well interfering I call it.'

'I'll have a word with her.'

'A word is not enough. I need her off my back.'

'I see.'

'And I want freedom to proceed as I see fit. Look, sir, we have two murders on our hands and Mullen has connections to both of them.'

'I am aware of that, but we do have to have sufficient evidence before we can make an arrest. As you know, circumstantial evidence is not sufficient.'

'How about blood?'

McPherson's eyes met his. 'Whose blood?'

'Mullen's. In the old barn, close to where the second body was found. It was on a piece of wood.'

'He often walked there. Maybe he cut himself on a previous occasion.'

'There're boot prints too. Same size as his feet.'

'You've checked his foot size?'

'They're on his record. Nine and a half.'

'Lots of men have feet that size.'

'It rained the afternoon the woman was murdered. The footprints must be fresh, the murderer's. Apart from the woman herself, there are no other recent prints.'

'Except for those of Baines, the woman who found the body,' McPherson said. 'And then the two uniformed officers and Mullen himself. The defence would make the most of that, him accompanying the officers, maybe intruding onto the crime scene.'

'The officers were experienced. They kept both of them at a distance. Look, sir, you can see where this is going, can't you?'

McPherson sat very still, rubbing his chin. He could see that Kingston was not going to let this go. 'I'm not sure I quite follow you, Andy.'

'Sir,' Kingston said, leaning forward. 'Suppose Mullen kills again while we are shilly-shallying around. What then?'

McPherson looked up sharply, conscious that his authority was being challenged. 'Shilly-shallying? Don't push your luck, Sergeant. Due process and checking things out thoroughly are not shilly-shallying!'

'Sorry, sir, I didn't mean it like that.' He paused, forcing himself to calm down. 'Look, sir, I am asking for two things. First for Holden not to be on my back, and secondly for your approval to arrest and charge Mullen. Then while I get the house searched from top to bottom and we ask more questions, the public is kept safe and he is prevented from doing a runner. If I'm wrong—'

McPherson cut across him. 'If you're wrong, Sergeant, then you'll be carrying the can. And let me tell you, if you are, the first thing the press will do is go raking through Mullen's well-documented history and they'll be coming up with headlines along the lines of "Hero wrongly arrested by bumbling police." So you had better be blooming well right.'

'I am right, sir.'

'In which case, carry on. But on your head be it.'

* * *

Mullen woke just after six a.m. after a wretched night and took the dog for a quick jog through the fields. He wanted not just to exercise Rex, but also to spring-clean his own brain.

He had to move out. That much was clear. Becca and he had barely spoken since their massive falling out two nights ago, but it was clear she needed her space. He certainly needed a comfortable bed and a less combative atmosphere. He had put that notice up on the board in the cinema on the spur of the moment, but how many people would even look at it? Finding digs would need much more than that. In truth, he wasn't sure he wanted to flatshare, and he would struggle to afford a place on his own, so maybe he would have to find another person who needed a house-sitter. Mind you, he had a dog now, and his last house-sit hadn't ended well. He stopped in his tracks and bent down low. Thinking about it made him feel suddenly nauseous.

'What do you think, Rex?'

The dog, who was starting to flag, looked up at him reproachfully. It was well past his breakfast time, and breakfast was very likely the only thing on his mind. Mullen tossed him a couple of treats that he had just discovered in the bottom of his pocket. The dog gobbled them up and looked at him. *Is that all?*

It was time to act. As soon as Mullen got back to the cottage, he got his tablet out and stuck an advert on the Nextdoor website. He had occasionally picked up things off it — logs and a really useful toolbox were the best — and it seemed an obvious place to advertise his availability as a house-sitter.

He had barely finished when Becca shuffled downstairs, clad in her dressing gown and with thoroughly scrambled hair. Mullen glanced at the cooker clock. It was seven a.m. This was, by recent standards, ludicrously early for Becca to be putting in an appearance.

There were several seconds of awkward silence. Mullen opened his mouth to say something, but she got there first.

'Sorry about the other night.' She walked across to him, and laid her hand on his shoulder. He jumped in surprise. She moved away and sat down at the opposite side of the table. 'You probably think I am a bit crazy when it comes to Alice's room, but I just cannot give it up to you.' She was breathing heavily and her clenched hands seemed to be engaged in a trial of strength with each other. 'You probably want to move out. God knows, I would if I were you. But, you see, I've made a decision. I need to try again to have a baby. But first I need to get well. I need to get fitter, lose weight, and I would like your help. Make sure I get up every morning and go out for a walk before breakfast. Eat healthily, stop filling up on crisps and chocolate and other crap. But you know me, I'm a backslider when it comes to that sort of thing, so I'll need your support.'

'I see,' he said. Though he didn't really. He had been poised to tell her that he was going to move out as soon as he had found somewhere else to stay, but she had aimed an arrow unerringly into his Achilles heel. *Help me!* Of course he would.

'So is that a "yes" or a "no?"' she pressed.

'A "yes."'

'Thank you, Doug. You're a good guy.'

'That's OK,' he said.

'However, there is one more thing.' She paused, dragging it out, her face a mask, but she was unable to stop a smile creeping across her features. 'The bathroom is no longer out of bounds, so you might want to have a shower.'

* * *

By nine a.m., both Mullen and Becca had showered (separately), eaten a very polite breakfast and then clambered into her car. She drove them to Wittenham Clumps, and together with Rex, they walked up both clumps and admired the countryside stretching out all around, green and fresh and full of promise. After the temporary truce established that morning, they were both on their best behaviour, each trying to demonstrate that they were more than able to put the rows and differences behind them, and yet each of them was conscious that one wrong word might cause a disastrous and possibly fatal relapse in their relationship.

They shared an unspoken understanding that being away from the confines of the cottage was a "good thing," so they delayed their return by stopping off for a coffee and croissant at the café at Benson Marina, where they talked about films they had seen and places they had been and anything else that kept them from straying into dangerous territory. Mullen tried to see it as a clearing of the air and a new beginning. He would stay for as long as she wanted him there. And if a house-sitting opportunity arose, he hoped to be able to take it without causing a crisis while also continuing to support her. He was convinced, above all, that they both needed more space.

'It must be my turn to cook,' Becca said unexpectedly as they drove home, and she was barely in the house before she began to prepare a vegetable soup. Mullen went outside and sat on a bench, keeping an eye on Rex. He had a few treats on him and was in the middle of teaching him a new trick when he heard the sound of cars approaching. They were moving fast. He straightened up and tensed with anxiety. The cars, sidelights gleaming, came into view. As they drew close, he could see that one of them was a marked police car. His heart plummeted.

Kingston and Royce got out, and behind them two uniformed officers. None of them were smiling. Kingston delivered the killer blow, marching up to Mullen while the others fanned out behind him as if expecting Mullen to make a run for it.

'Douglas Mullen, I am arresting you on suspicion of murder. I must caution you that you do not have to say or do anything, but anything that you do say may be taken down and may be used in evidence against you. Do you understand?'

Mullen stood there, unable to take it all in. Royce moved forward and handcuffed him, and before he knew it the two uniforms were driving him away while the detectives remained in the doorway of the cottage, talking to Becca. It was as quick and simple as that. One minute he was contemplating a new and healthier relationship with Becca, and the next a future behind bars.

* * *

When DS Kingston told Becca they needed to search her house and that she would need to find somewhere else to stay until they had finished, she stared at him in disbelief.

'But this is my house,' she said. 'It's where I sleep. Where I have all my clothes and . . .'

She dribbled to a full stop, and he — quite kindly — assured her that he understood, and that hopefully she would be able to return the next day. In the meantime, did she have a friend she could stay with?

'What about the dog?' she said. And he stared at her with an expression that she recognized all too well from her working life — the look that says someone has just asked the most bizarre question.

She packed a single case, put Rex in the car and drove off without a word. Two miles down the road was a kennels. She knew nothing about it, but the board outside was freshly painted in tasteful colours, and either side of the words "Jane's Kennels" were silhouetted images of a spaniel and a poodle. They were rather cute. If Jane liked cute dogs, she would surely take a Westiepoodle for a couple of nights.

Jane turned out to be middle-aged and distressingly jolly, which was the last thing Becca wanted. A sour-faced eighty-year-old complaining about the thoughtlessness of people who give no advance warning would have been much easier to bear. But eventually Becca broke free, drove down the road, pulled in at the first gateway she spotted and burst into tears.

What was she to do? Or rather who could she ask for help? One name popped into her head, and before she could have second thoughts, she found his contact details on her mobile and rang him. It went into voicemail and she left a distressed message saying that she had been turfed out of her house by the police and Mullen was in jail and she needed somewhere to stay. Then she sank back in her seat and wondered why on earth she had asked Leo Francombe of all people — the man who had fathered her baby — for help. She didn't especially blame him for the pregnancy, only that it had caused him to drop her like a hot brick. Quite what was going on in his home life she had no idea, except that a few weeks previously he had rung her and asked for her forgiveness. She had tried not to be unkind, but she had made it clear she had no intention of letting him wheedle his way back into her life and bed.

So why was she calling him now? Desperation was one obvious answer. But there was another one too. The fact was that he owed her, and she knew she could manipulate him. She wasn't proud of that thought, but she could use his guilt over poor little Alice to force him to help her.

She closed her eyes. She suddenly felt very tired. He would be working and unlikely to respond to her message for hours. That was Leo all over. Hard to contact unless he wanted to be. She fell asleep, the phone clasped in her hand. How long she slept she had no idea, except that she was suddenly awake, aware that her phone was vibrating, signalling the arrival of a text. It was from him. *Life is busy and complicated. Meet at Oxford Spires Hotel 7 p.m. Leo x.*

She didn't like the "x" and didn't like the fact that he seemed to be getting in his excuses first. But she replied without hesitation. *Thank you. See you then.*

* * *

She arrived at the hotel early, so she went to the bar and bought a gin and tonic, which she took to a table in the corner. A copy of *The Times* had been abandoned there, so she hid behind it. It was definitely not her political cup of tea, but she didn't want to have to fend off businessmen looking to liven up their evening. She knew how that normally ended, and had no desire to repeat the experience.

She had almost finished her drink when she sensed someone standing over her. 'Can I get you anything, madam?' For a moment she thought it was the barman, but when she looked up Leo was standing there, in an expensive suit and striped shirt (no tie). She almost burst into tears.

'Soft, please.'

He was back a couple of minutes later with what he assured her was a mocktail and a whisky for himself. He took a sip, then extracted a small card from his pocket and pushed it across the table to her.

'What's that?' Though she knew very well.

'Room key. I've booked you in for the night.'

She glared at him, but before she could say anything, he anticipated her. 'You can't stay at mine. I've got a new relationship going now, and you appearing out of the woodwork wouldn't be helpful. So I've booked you in for dinner, bed and breakfast, and if they don't let you go home tomorrow then just say so and I'll cover that too.' He paused, meeting her gaze. 'It's the least I can do and—'

'Does she know about baby Alice?'

He took another sip and savoured the taste, all the time watching her with his startling blue eyes. 'It's early days, and I'm not sure she needs to yet.'

'Does she know about me at all — or the others?'

'We have agreed that there are certain things that neither of us needs to share.'

'So that's a big fat "no!" then. I am not even history. I am excised from the story of your life for ever.' She knew she wasn't being fair. But she wanted to punish him.

'Becca, is there anything else I can do for you?' he said, before knocking back the rest of his whisky, apparently unhurt by her jibes.

'No,' she replied.

'I want to say something,' he said firmly. 'You may not wish to hear it from me, but even so I ask you to listen.' He paused, waiting until he was sure he had her attention. 'The pain will pass. Not soon. Not in a single dramatic moment, but over time. You will not forget Alice, nor will you want to. But the pain will subside.'

'Is that it?'

'No, Becca, that is not it. There is one more thing. I believe you should return to work. They need you, Becca, and I am sure you need them too. Friends, and a purpose in life.'

She wanted to argue with him, ask him how the hell he could know about her pain, which sometimes gripped her so tightly that she could hardly move or breathe, but instead she began to weep. The tears descended softly and silently, and for so long that when she finally brought herself back under control and had wiped her face dry, she discovered that he had gone.

Except that he hadn't run out on her. He was standing near the bar talking to someone, a man of similar build, over six feet tall and broad of shoulder. Similarly aged too, wearing navy chinos, a pale blue shirt and a lightweight casual jacket.

Both men were looking at her. How long for? She felt exposed, the prize exhibit at an auction, and straightened her back as they started towards her.

'Becca, this is James Elworthy,' Leo said. 'A fellow consultant. We read medicine together at the university and were rivals for a rugby blue when we were young and fit. James, this is Becca Baines. A top-class A & E nurse.'

'Good to meet you, Becca.' He stretched out a long arm to shake her hand, studying her with curious brown eyes. 'Although I do wonder if we haven't bumped into each other before.'

She shook her head. 'I don't think so.'

'Some fundraiser maybe?'

'Not that I recall.'

'Ah well, it *is* nice to meet you. I gather from Leo you're going through a tough time.'

She started. 'Oh, really?' Had Leo been talking about her and Mullen, or the baby? The former she hoped.

'Can I buy you another drink? I have a few minutes to kill while I wait for my dinner companion to arrive, and Leo was telling me that he has to go home shortly.'

'Thank you. But I think I need a shower.'

'Of course.' There was an awkward pause, then he added, 'You do definitely look familiar.'

She shrugged and turned to Leo, saying in a very un-Becca like way, 'Thank you for your kindness.' Then she picked up her overnight bag and headed off in search of her room, resisting the urge to glance back and see if they were still watching her, or had already dismissed her for more interesting things.

* * *

Detective Superintendent McPherson wasn't surprised when his door banged open. He had known it would only be a matter of time before Holden came storming in.

'What the hell is going on? Why wasn't I kept informed?' She stood there, hands on hips. She was steaming.

'Susan,' he said, his voice as smooth as brushed velvet. 'I understand you had an appointment at the hospital yesterday. Is everything all right?'

She was momentarily thrown off balance, surprised that the information had filtered that far up the chain of command. But she ignored the question. 'Why the hell did you let Andy arrest Doug?'

'Doug? Now there's the problem in a nutshell. You call him Doug. A friend. Indeed far too much of a friend for you to be able to view him dispassionately.'

'He's proved himself in the past. I trust him.'

'Sit down, Susan.' His voice was suddenly as cold and sharp as a steel knife. 'Now!'

She hesitated for three or four seconds. Then, somewhat to his surprise, she sat. 'There isn't enough evidence.'

'There is plenty of evidence.'

'Mostly circumstantial.'

'Some is circumstantial, but the problem for Mullen is that there is now sufficient evidence for us to view him as our prime suspect.'

'What evidence?'

McPherson had a sudden realization that she hadn't been told about it. That Kingston and the others had been keeping the details to themselves. Had Wozniak been kept out of the loop too? The word around the station was that she had already allied herself to Holden. Were they both gay, or was it just that they were both women?

'We now have compelling forensic evidence.'

'Such as?'

'You don't need to know the details. You're no longer involved with the case. In fact you should never have got yourself involved in the first place.'

'Doug Mullen is a good guy.'

'A good guy?' McPherson exploded with laughter. 'Is that your professional assessment?'

Holden could feel herself losing her grip on the case, and even reality. She tried to recover. 'All I mean is that I know him and he couldn't be the murderer.'

'Anyone can be a murderer. All it takes are the right circumstances, the right motivation and a loss of control. You know that.'

'Not Doug,' she said plaintively.

McPherson stood up. He was a big man, who knew how to intimidate people. 'This meeting is over. And you, Detective, are on leave for the next two weeks. We can call it sick leave if you like, but I want you out of the station. You're a danger to the investigation. If you're still hanging around in half an hour, you'll be on a disciplinary. Now get out of my sight.'

There was no option. No point in arguing. Holden stood up.

'And one more thing, Susan. If you try getting young Krystyna to do your dirty work, then it'll be curtains on her career before it has even got off the ground. Do I make myself clear.'

She gave him an icy stare. 'I understand.'

'I understand, sir!'

'Sir.'

She turned and left the room.

* * *

Holden meant what she said to McPherson about keeping clear of Wozniak. McPherson's threat had hit home. The young constable would have a hard enough time as it was without her making it any worse. Which is why it was a surprise for her to come out of her toilet cubicle and find Wozniak waiting for her. Her face was pale and she was trembling.

'I am so sorry, ma'am. I should have warned you, but I didn't know. You see, they sidelined me—'

Holden raised a hand. 'Not your fault, Krystyna. Listen, it's not a good idea to be seen talking to me, so just get back to your desk and do your job.'

'But, ma'am—'

Holden opened her handbag and removed a biro and a tissue. She wrote her private contact details on the tissue and passed it over. 'In extremis. But whatever you do, don't let on.'

Wozniak took the tissue and held her hand out for the biro. She tore the tissue in half, wrote her number down and handed the half-tissue and pen back.

Holden found herself suddenly very unsteady. She grabbed the edge of the wash basin as an unexpected wave of gratitude swept over her. Here was someone at the beginning of her career choosing to support her when it would have been much wiser not to. She felt like crying, she felt like giving her a hug, but she did no such things. Instead she leaned forward and whispered, 'Now go, before, before . . .' *Before I weaken.*

'Yes, ma'am.'

* * *

It was the first time Mullen had been properly imprisoned. Of course, he had had his brushes with the law in his youth. As a young runaway sleeping on the streets of London, he had been moved on by the police a few times. If a homeless guy called Bill had not taken him under his wing and persuaded him to go back home, then very likely he would have got into greater trouble. A couple of years after that, he had spent a night in a cell after making a drunken exhibition of himself, but was released the next morning with a friendly warning. He had repeated the experience a few weeks later, and this time he had only been released after a copper had punched him so hard he had cracked a rib — a not-so-friendly warning that (this time) Mullen had heeded.

But being on remand with no bail was a very different kettle of fish. Though it was something he would barely admit to himself, let alone to anyone else, that first night he had slept badly as fear and anxiety rippled through him. What if he was convicted? What would it be like — to be locked up for years and years, and deprived of the few friends he had gained? Most alarmingly, what if Becca gave up on him?

The second night had been better. He slept through the night, only waking when Charlie, who slept in the bunk below him, prodded him in the side of his chest and told him to 'stop effing snoring.'

Mullen didn't mind. Charlie, he had decided, was OK. He could have been shut up with a much worse companion. Charlie knew the ropes in prison — and everything there was to know about burglary — and as long as Mullen let him call the shots, they got on fine.

'I'm innocent,' he had told Charlie that first night as they lay in their bunks, but the only response he received was a loud guffaw and an 'ain't we all!'

CHAPTER 6

It's not as if it was all carefully planned. It was more a case of things just happening. You could say things fell into place easily — maybe too easily. Julie had really got under my skin so I arranged to meet her one evening. I rang her on my burner phone because I didn't trust her. 'I'd like to buy you supper one evening as a thank you for your kindness to Kat,' I said. It was a load of flannel. She knew and I knew. But she also knew what she wanted. 'There's a good film at the Ultimate Picture Palace,' she said. 'Maybe we can do that as well.' I said yes. The more I gave her what she wanted, the more cooperative she would be. But then Murphy's law kicked in. I had a serious work problem that I needed to sort out, so I had to text her and tell her so, but I promised I would try and see her later.

In the end the problem took longer to sort out than I expected and I got to the Cowley Road five minutes before the film she was watching was due to finish. So I parked and waited. She came out, but there was a guy talking to her. I felt a flash of jealousy, I admit. This was my evening with her. But she seemed to see him off and then she checked her phone — I had just sent her a message — and she looked around and saw me and came scurrying across the road.

She was a bit cool to begin with, punishing me, making me pay for messing up her evening. I got that. But by the time we had grabbed a Chinese takeaway from a place up the road, she had started to thaw out. We ate in the car, but when I headed out of town, she began to whine and said she just wanted to go home. 'First things first,' I said. 'I'll find somewhere quiet where we can hole up for a while, then I'll drop you back at your door.'

'Take me home,' she said, as if she were in charge. 'I've changed my mind.'

'I just need to talk to you,' I lied.

That made her laugh, a rather dirty laugh it was too. 'I've heard that one before. Just remember the haircut was free, but sex isn't.'

'Of course,' I said. 'I remember that. I remember that very, very well.'

'One hundred,' she said. 'Card or cash.'

* * *

Becca slept remarkably well that night despite all the thoughts that were flying around inside her head. She had been pre-scribed sleeping pills after the loss of Alice, but abandoned them after a few days because she wanted to feel the pain of loss, not numb herself to it. Nonetheless, she had resisted the urge to throw the rest of them away. Instead, she had kept them tucked away in her handbag just in case she needed them. As she sat on her bed that evening eating a solitary dinner ordered from room service, she came to the realization that on this occasion she really did need them. So she put on her nightie, brushed her teeth and took a double dose. She wanted oblivion and that seemed to be the best way to achieve it.

The following morning she didn't go down for breakfast until nearly nine a.m. She sat herself in a corner determined — after all, Leo was paying — to eat her fill. Money was getting tight, and if she had to spend the whole day killing time in Oxford while the scene-of-crime people snooped into every corner of her house, then she ought not to splash out on things just because she was bored or hungry. The fact was — as Leo had gently pointed out — she needed to get back to work, and not just for emotional reasons.

She was pondering these thoughts when James Elworthy suddenly appeared. 'May I join you?' he said and sat down without waiting for an answer. 'Sleep well? I knocked on your door at about nine thirty last night. I was hoping we might have a chat.'

She stared at him. The coffee and food had helped her slough off her torpor, but his unexpected appearance was like a sharp jab in the ribs. She felt anger rise inside her.

'Why did you pretend you didn't know me?' He spoke calmly, softly, a man in command of himself.

'Can't you guess?' she hissed.

'I would have looked after you.'

'No thanks then, and no thanks now.'

He took a sip from the cup of coffee he had brought with him and placed it, very carefully, on the table.

'Leo and I have been talking, and we both think it is time for you to move on.'

'You've been talking about me, have you?' She was on the verge of exploding. What right did Leo have to share her confidences with anyone, let alone James Elworthy?

'Only because we care about you.'

She was seething. But he either didn't notice or didn't care. 'The fact is you need to shed this Mullen chap from your life. He sounds like a thoroughly bad sort and attaching yourself to him is the worst thing you could possibly do.'

'His name is Doug. And he is a very good friend.'

But Elworthy ploughed on, apparently oblivious. 'If you really want a baby — and Leo tells me you do — then that is easy enough to arrange these days. If you need a donor, then Leo or I would happily oblige.'

'How very kind of you.' She stood up, grabbed her bag and as she walked past him knocked his cup over, spraying coffee across the white cloth and his immaculate blue-and-white-striped shirt. She heard him curse, but she didn't look back. In in a public place like this, she felt pretty safe. He couldn't hurt her here, not like he had in the past.

* * *

It was a huge relief to be home after only one night in the hotel. She had been dreading having to stay on and having either James or Leo turning up, knocking on her door, all charm on the surface but with a secret agenda lying barely concealed underneath. It was late afternoon and surprisingly cold. Despite her various layers of clothing, Becca shivered, but it wasn't just because of the temperature. It was impossible not to think of Mullen stuck in a cell. He wasn't the sort of guy who went around killing women. She knew him well enough to know that, and yet there he was and here she was. And here too was Rex, his ridiculously cute dog, trotting along at her feet, as if he had taken on the duty of keeping her both safe and on track with her new health regime.

Rex was leading now, and she knew all too well where he was heading — to the old barn where the woman in the green coat had been lying. Mullen had often walked him that way. She wondered if the police tape would still be up, with a couple of uniforms standing guard against the likes of her, but as the structure came into view she could see they had gone. She felt a spurt of anxiety. The last time she had been here, the wretched woman had been lying there, and Mullen had opened his mouth right next to the pair of officers, and after that one thing had led to another.

Rex whined. She should have kept him on his lead. Suppose he caught the scent of something, a rabbit maybe, and flew off across the field in vain pursuit? Would he return to her if she called? The dog whined again and galloped off at speed. She called after him. 'Here, Rex, here!'

But the dog wasn't stopping, and he was soon taking a shortcut through a hedge. By the time Becca had made her way to the gateway in the corner of the field, she could hear yelping. She swore out loud. The police must still be there. And sure enough, there was a figure bending down and playing with the dog. 'I'm so sorry,' she called out. The figure, dressed in dark trousers and a black hooded anorak, stood up, cradling the dog in his arms. 'Sorry,' Becca apologized again. 'I hope he didn't—'

'Hello, Becca.' The woman — for it was most definitely a woman — smiled.

'You!' Alarm and anger fought for dominance.

'Me.' DI Holden let Rex jump down.

'I thought you lot had finished here.'

'They have.'

'So, what's going on?'

'I've been taken off the case.' Holden pulled her hood off her head and shook her hair free. It was tousled, not something Becca would have associated with her. 'Two weeks of compulsory leave while they decide what to do with me.'

'Why's that?'

'Because I don't believe for a minute that Doug killed anyone.'

Becca looked at her. Doug trusted Holden. He talked enough about her, that was for sure. Occasionally Becca had felt ridiculously jealous, yet it was patently obvious that Holden and he would never be more than friends. That was as plain as a lump on a log, as her grandmother used to say.

'How do I know you aren't just saying that?'

'You don't.'

They fell silent then. Rex was sitting down, scratching behind his ear, suddenly bored with all the chat.

'I need to get back,' Becca said eventually. 'The dog's not eaten since breakfast.'

'Neither have I,' Holden said.

* * *

'I hope they didn't mess up your house too much?' Holden gestured around the room. It looked, as Becca's mother would have disparaged, "lived in." The two rugs needed a vacuum or a beating, the daffodils in a vase on the window were wilting for lack of water, and she could see a spider's web delicately spread along the top of the front window.

'It's eggs and bacon, or bacon and eggs. With toast.'

'That sounds fine.'

'I meant to call in at the supermarket, but you know how it is.'

'Do you mind if I use your toilet?'

'Be my guest.' It would have been churlish to refuse, even though she really wanted her house and her privacy back. She couldn't help noticing that Holden took an awful long time upstairs. Was she snooping too?

Eventually, she reappeared and they were soon sitting down opposite each other, eating with a will.

'Delicious,' Holden ("call me Susan") said as she wiped her plate clean with a third piece of toast. 'Tell me, Becca, am I right in thinking that Doug still sleeps on the sofa bed?' They had been having a woman-to-woman talk while they worked their way through the brunch, and it had been pretty trivial until Holden slipped this in.

'That's our business,' Becca said.

'Is he sleeping with you or not, Becca? If you want me to help, I need honest answers to my questions.'

Becca took a piece of half-eaten toast from her plate and tossed it to Rex. 'No. I think he'd like to, but I'm not ready.'

'Is he often out at night? Stays away sometimes, does he?'

'What the hell are you implying?' She was on a knife edge, defensive on Doug's behalf.

'I think you know what I am asking.'

'I lost my baby. Stillborn. I expect he may have told you. Anyway, he has been ridiculously caring since then. Cooking, cleaning, always coming back home. I really can't remember him staying out all night. By contrast I've been either mon-osyllabic or a harridan.'

'So he's maybe been getting sexually frustrated?'

'What do you mean? Are you blaming me for denying him sex and so turning him into a sexual predator?'

'No. Well, not exactly, but I have to consider every pos-sibility. And the fact is, he did try to pick up Julie Baxter at the cinema.'

'He spoke to her. She dropped something on the floor. He picked it up. Chatted to her. Bought her a drink. But that hardly makes him a murderer.'

'Come on, Becca. A woman who drops a handkerchief on the floor, a man who gallantly picks it up. It's straight out of a Mills & Boon novel.'

'That doesn't mean it isn't true.'

'Stop deluding yourself. Doug Mullen tried to pick up Julie Baxter and later that evening she ended up dead.'

Becca banged her fists on the table. 'No. I know him. He's not a sexual predator. You make it sound like he went out looking for easy sex. What he was actually doing was escaping from me. I wasn't nice to be with. God only knows why he didn't move out ages ago, but the fact is he stuck by me. I wish now that he hadn't, then this would never have happened.'

'And the woman in the green coat, the one who died, it was you who found her?'

'Yes. That time it was me trying to get away from him.'

'When, precisely, was this?'

'I told your officers.'

'Tell me.'

She shut her eyes and tried to think. 'We had breakfast together. He had been out really late the night before, so he was still in his pyjamas. We ate, and after that I went out for a walk. I suppose it was about nine a.m. When I got to the old barn, I found the dead woman. I hadn't got my mobile with me, so I came back as quickly as I could and rang 999. When your officers arrived, I led them there. Doug came with us, and when we got there, he was clearly stunned to see this woman in a green coat lying on the ground.'

'I have to ask you this. Do you think he could possibly have been putting on an act?'

'No. Definitely not.'

'And before all this happened, had he talked about the woman in a green coat who he met at the Turf Tavern in Oxford?'

'Oh yes, he had been thoroughly taken in by her. Couldn't work out who she was or even what she wanted. But if you're thinking whether he made her up, then really you're barking up the wrong tree. Mullen is definitely not a devious killer in an Agatha Christie story.'

'But Doug insists that the woman he met in the pub was much older than the woman you found in the barn. That *is* like something out of an Agatha Christie story.'

'Yes.' Becca had been thinking about this a lot. She had a theory, which she wasn't sure if she fully believed or not, but as Holden stood up, indicating that she was about to leave, it felt like now or never. 'Look, Susan, this may seem like a long shot, but you can really do an awful lot with a good wig, plus some clever make-up. I shared a house with a girl who did that in the film business. She made me up for a party once, and no one guessed who I was until I started to talk. My point is that an actor could carry that off.'

'I'm not sure. Would Doug really have been taken in? My impression is that he's good at spotting things that aren't quite right.'

'He laughed when I suggested it to him. But my point is that he wasn't actually with her that long. When he arrived, she asked him to buy her a drink, which she downed almost immediately. Very soon after that, she asked him for a coffee, and when he returned from the bar with it she had gone.'

They both fell silent — Becca because she felt drained, and Holden because she was sizing up whether and how she should ask a final question. She felt sorry for Becca and rather liked her, and yet she was still a policewoman seeking answers.

'Tell me,' she said very softly. 'Do you think it is possible that Mullen did it?'

Becca looked across at her inquisitor. She felt as though she were backed up against a wall. Of course it was possible. Anything was possible. But she wasn't going to say so out loud. Instead, she gave the briefest of nods and stood up, trying to brush off the terrible realization that she had just betrayed her dearest friend.

Holden left a few minutes later, wrapped in a mantle of silence. Becca watched her go, wondering if she really could help. Would any of the powers that be listen to her now — even if she did discover something? Did Holden have any influence left at the station? And was it sensible to put her trust in the woman? She couldn't get rid of the feeling that the case, that is to say Doug, was a lost cause.

* * *

Holden had only just left Baines when her phone rang. She answered it and pulled over into the first gateway she saw so she could concentrate. It was Wozniak. 'I've tracked Tapper down. To Slough.'

'Do you have an address?'

'Not exactly.' Wozniak went silent. There were car noises in the background, and a baby wailing. Then the phone went silent too. Holden waited. Surely Wozniak hadn't been ringing from just outside the station? Two or three minutes passed, and then the phone rang again.

'Sorry. Look, Bob Tapper does paved front drives at people's houses. Not dodgy tarmac ones, but those with block paving. Works mostly for a company called Drives Alive. They mostly cover the Home Counties north of London. He is, how would you say, a gun for hire for them.'

Holden smiled at her English. 'Not literally, I hope.'

But Wozniak wasn't listening. 'Look, I am under pressure. I have already had Andy blowing down my neck this morning, and that horrible Royce keeps looking at me, so—'

'Breathing down your neck, not blowing.'

'Ah, yes, breathing. Thank you. Anyway, you understand that I am very busy . . .'

'Yes, of course. I'll go and take a snoop around myself. It'll be good for me.'

'If I hear anything else, I'll text.'

'Thank you, Krystyna.'

'No worries, ma'am.'

* * *

Drives Alive were easy enough to track down. They had an address in what turned out to be a grotty industrial estate on the fringes of Slough. The estate consisted of two rows of grey featureless blocks, and Drives Alive were situated at the far end on the right. There were a couple of well-worn cars parked at the front, and a dirty white pick-up with *Drives Alive* splashed along the side. Holden pulled up and went in through a distinctly flimsy door.

'Can I help?' A young woman with hair that was streaked pink and blonde looked up. She had been working on her nails.

'I'm interested in having a new drive installed.'

'That's what we do.'

'I got chatting with one of your men the other day and he seemed OK.'

'All our workmen are OK. They are fully trained and very experienced,' the woman said, getting into her sales spiel. 'I can assure you that they will do a very good job for you. If you give me your details, I can arrange for someone to come and give you a quotation.' She blew on her nails, then swore. 'I've bloody smudged them.'

'He said his name was Bob.' Holden frowned. 'Something like hammer, no, not hammer. Now what was it? That's right. Got it. Tapper. Bob Tapper. Or was it Rob? I can't remember. I think I prefer Rob.' She laughed. 'Still, it's not my name, is it, it's his.'

The woman looked at her, suddenly uncertain as to how to respond. 'So, madam . . . do you want to give me your details?'

Holden smiled the smile of the innocent. 'Sure.' The name she gave was the name of her primary school teacher and the address was a house she had identified on the fringe of town that needed one hell of a makeover at the front.

'So, where's Bob working today?'

'It won't necessarily be him who gives you your quotation.'

'Look, sweetie, if I'm gonna put work your way, then I want to go and see the quality of your work, so if you just tell me where he's working, then I can go and check the quality of his paving, and if I am happy, then he can claim his bonus for finding the business another client. I expect that's how it works, isn't it?'

She nodded slowly. 'We don't usually . . .'

Holden pulled out her wallet, removed two tenners and laid them on the table, with her hand placed firmly on top. 'What, you want a cut too, do you?' Her voice hissed. When she needed it, intimidation was second nature. 'Will this help you to decide? You could go to a nail bar and get yourself done properly. But first I need to know where Bob is working. So, my dear, you've five seconds to make a decision. After that, these notes go back in my wallet. Yes or no?'

* * *

Holden drove like the wind. She didn't trust the pinky blonde further than she could spit. She'd taken the money soon enough, squirrelling it into her bag, but that didn't mean she wouldn't give Tapper a ring as soon as she was out the door. It was a ten-minute drive maximum. Even if Tapper wanted to skedaddle, he'd be hard pushed to clear all his stuff up and get away before she arrived.

Of course, sod's law meant that there was bound to be a delay — and some idiot in a lorry duly obliged by managing to make a dog's dinner of a turn down a narrow alley with cars parked along both sides. But once she was past him, spitting fury, she found herself sailing free and unimpeded. She pulled up outside Number Sixty-six just as a man in a red baseball cap and black overalls was about to get into his van. She screamed to a halt behind him, blocking him in.

'What the hell's going on?'

'I've come to admire your paving.'

'It's not finished yet.'

'So I see.' She looked around. 'I'm thinking about getting a new drive myself. But I like to do a spot check before I hand over any money.'

'If you think I believe that, you must take me for a complete fool. Who are you? Working for the tax office? Chasing poor buggers like me who are just trying to earn an honest living?'

'I'm chasing people who beat the shit out of their wives.'

The penny dropped, and the bravado disappeared like smoke in a hurricane.

Holden held up her ID and waited.

'We split up ages ago. Water under the bridge.'

'Not seen her since?'

'No. She moved. No idea where she lives.'

'You've moved too.'

'It's cheaper out here.'

'It's much cheaper up north than it is here.'

'I've got work here. Anyway, what exactly do you want? If it's about the wife, I don't know where she is. She just packed her bags and left.'

'She went to live in Oxford, with her mum. Not so far from here. Trying to start a new life, just like you. And then the other night she turned up dead in a ditch just outside the city.'

Tapper shut his eyes, then opened them again. He put his hand over his face. A man in pain — or a man pretending to be in pain? Holden wasn't sure, but she had a strong feeling. 'We didn't end well,' Tapper said at last. 'But she didn't deserve that.'

'Deserve what?'

'If she ended up dead in a ditch and you've come looking for me, I imagine we're talking murder.'

Holden nodded. 'So, when did you last see her?'

'Not since she left me.'

'You're sure about that?'

'I'm not saying anything more without a solicitor present. I know what the likes of you do, getting people to say stuff.'

'If you've not done anything, you've nothing to fear.'

He laughed. 'Do I look like I was born yesterday? You decide I'm guilty, then you try and find the evidence to prove it.'

'All I need to know is where you were on the night of the fifteenth of March?'

He leaned deep into his van and a moment later re-emerged with a battered black book in his hand. He flicked through it until he found the date and looked across at Holden. 'I was working in High Wycombe all day.'

'What about the evening?'

'Had a meal in a Wetherspoons pub. Can't remember its name. Had a few drinks too, because I was going to crash at a mate's house. But someone got a bit lairy, thought I was eyeing up his girl, and we ended up in a bit of a fracas.'

'What sort of fracas?'

He paused, allowing a smirk to creep across his face. 'The sort of fracas that involves the local police sticking their noses in. It kinda spoiled my evening.'

* * *

It was early morning and Becca was out walking when she remembered it. Now that she had set her mind on getting fit for another baby, nothing was going to stop her, and of course there was also the dog to be walked now that Doug had been detained. She would have to go back to work soon too. Leo had gently prodded her in that direction, and for all his faults, she knew he was right. But she couldn't just leave Doug to it. Then what? Just wait and hope that Susan Holden came up with something that proved he was innocent?

Then the rain began to fall, no mere shower, but a raining-stair-rods storm, just like it had the day Doug met that woman at the Turf. He had come back soaked through, and — she suddenly remembered — he had been carrying a book the woman had left behind. He had laughed, describing how Rex had been lying on top of it as if he were guarding the crown jewels. Doug had slapped it down on the table, so where was it now?

By the time she got home, she too was soaked through, so she had a shower, got into her nightwear, even though it was only 7 p.m., and had a supper of poached eggs on toast. Then she went and looked through the small chest of drawers in which Mullen kept most of his worldly goods. And there it was — a paperback with curled edges, still slightly damp: *Somebody's Baby*. The very title caught her by the throat. She read the blurb on the back: *A baby girl is abandoned in a churchyard, mother unknown, and is adopted by a childless couple. In adulthood she goes in search of her biological mother. Will she succeed?*

Of course she will succeed. That was obvious, but Becca felt compelled to read it nevertheless. It was less than 200 pages in a generous sized font. It wouldn't take long. So she made herself a mug of tea, stretched out on Doug's sofa bed and began to read. She was halfway through before she realized something. From time to time, someone had underlined a word in pencil, only lightly, but it was clear enough. She stopped and stared at the one on page ninety-seven: "help." She looked back, starting at the beginning: "please," "please," "help," "please", "please," "help." She turned the pages, past ninety-seven and beyond. These words were highlighted wherever they occurred. And then, two pages from the end, she came across the final underlined word: "me."

Becca looked down at her hands. Her fingers had balled up into her palms. She let out a gasp of air, suddenly aware that she had been holding her breath. Was this the work of the woman Doug had talked about? It had to be. The woman he had met in the pub, who he had talked to, who had been there one minute and gone the next. She had left this book behind. It was a plea for help, but who on earth was she, and how on earth could Becca hope to find her?

The dog was whining. She levered herself to her feet, walked over to the door and let him out. He disappeared into the bushes while she tried to think.

She ought to prioritize seeing Doug. So, ring Althea Potter and organize that, pronto. See if he was all right. What a stupid thing to think! He was hardly going to be all right. But she needed to talk to him, ask him questions.

Hopefully, the police were searching for the dead woman's name. If they succeeded, then surely someone else might rise to the surface as prime suspect. But how many resources were they going to put into finding out who she was? As far as they were concerned, the woman was dead and Doug Mullen had done it. That was what mattered.

So, what about the woman in the pub? Who on earth was she? The problem was that the police wouldn't be interested in investigating her at all because they were convinced that the woman in the pub was the woman who had ended up dead only a few fields away. Why look any further? Case closed.

* * *

'Doug, you look like shit.'

Becca had wondered how to approach him. *Be gentle, take it all nice and easy, in fact don't be yourself.* But as soon as she saw him, all her best intentions flew out the window.

His mouth creased into half a smile. 'You look . . . hot!'

It was such a non-Doug expression that she too broke into a grin. *Hot!* She felt a frisson of pleasure, despite the situation. She had made an effort, washed her hair, tried on several different dresses before reverting to her favourite purple one, with a wide belt. She had put on her sun and moon earrings after much debate with Rex, who had been watching her with a cocked head, aware that something was going on. Doug had once commented on them — favourably. She wondered if he would remember.

She wanted to lean across and take his hand, but she had been warned about that. So they sat staring at each other, like two teenagers sizing each other up at a school dance.

'I want to help you.' She spoke quietly, as if such words might cause her to be forcibly ejected for planning a jail break.

'Good.'

'The woman in the pub. Tell me anything and everything you know about her.'

'I have told the police,' he said gently.

'Don't be an idiot,' she hissed. 'They aren't going to do anything. Why would they? They think she's the dead woman.'

'I trust Susan Holden.'

'She's been taken off the case, Doug. She came round and spoke to me. It was kind of her. We had a nice chat, but frankly she hasn't got any power anymore.'

She saw his shoulders slump and realized how much he must have been relying on her to come to his aid. 'Tell me about Kat, Doug.'

He sank his head in his hands.

'Kat with a "K," wasn't it?'

'She may have made it up.'

'Snap out of it, Doug. We don't have much time. You thought she was in her sixties, yes?'

'Grey hair, a few streaks of white. Nice blue eyes and a slightly lop-sided mouth. Her skin was smooth, but creased at the corners of her mouth and eyes. I know what you said about your friend who was into film make-up, but I really do think Kat was that sort of age.'

'What else? What did she say? Do you think she lived in Oxford? How did she get to the pub? Why that pub?'

'She said she used to go there when she was a student. She said the junior common room bar was cheaper, but sometimes she just wanted to get out.'

'She didn't say which college?'

He sighed. 'I'm not sure she could remember. I got the idea that she had some form of dementia.'

'Or maybe she was on some sort of strong medication. That can make people forgetful.'

He shrugged. 'You'll know more about that than me.'

'Did she mention catching a bus or a taxi?'

'No. I saw her walking, almost running actually, across Catte Street and into New College Lane. It was pouring with rain.'

'Anything else that struck you, Doug? Anything at all?' She was beginning to lose hope. None of this helped.

'She said she felt things. Said she could smell smoke on Rex's fur.'

'Yes, I remember you telling me. But as I said, she could easily have been making that up. She could have read about it in the newspaper. When it all happened, you became quite a local celebrity for a day or two.'

A shadow loomed over the table. 'One more minute!' The voice was gravel-deep.

'What else, Doug? Something, anything.'

'She had no money. I bought her a gin and tonic, and then a coffee, and then . . .' He paused, as something clicked. 'She had a mobile phone. I looked back when I went to order the coffee and she was looking at a mobile phone. The next time I looked, when I returned with the coffee, she had disappeared.'

'Remind me. What time did you arrange to meet?'

'Eleven forty-five.' He leaned forward. 'You've got to find her, Becca.'

'Time's up.' For a second time a shadow loomed across the table.

Becca looked up. The warder had a face that could have dashed a thousand ships upon the rocks of destruction.

'That's a shame.' She looked up, smiling her sweetest smile, and stretched across the table to try and squeeze Mullen's hand, but the warder intervened.

'Stop that!'

So she stopped and watched as he was led away. 'Love you!' she called suddenly. The cow couldn't stop her doing that.

CHAPTER 7

'*Time for your medicine.*'

I looked up. Lily was standing in front of me, a small syringe in her hand. I have never liked syringes. Mother told me that I used to scream the house down when I was a child. But the syringe that Lily was holding didn't have a needle. I am grateful that he has arranged that for me. This syringe is like that which mothers use nowadays when their children have a temperature and they need a carefully measured dose of medicine. Ngung explained that to me. '*Just slip it into your mouth and squeeze,*' she had said. '*Calpol is pink, but yours is white.*' I would have preferred pink. I mentioned it once to him, but he had laughed and said they didn't get a choice of colour. My medicine was white. That was all there was to it.

'*Where's Ngung?*' I said suddenly. I preferred Ngung. Was it wrong to prefer Ngung to Lily?

'*On holiday,*' Lily said. '*She hasn't had one for a long time.*'

I thought about that as she went and put the medicine and syringe back in their cupboard. It hadn't occurred to me that Ngung might need a holiday. It was very nice here. A big house, a big garden, a swing seat, even a swimming pool. But no seaside. Perhaps that was where Ngung had gone. To the seaside.

'*Shall we go and pick some flowers?*' Lily said. '*There are lots of them.*'

'What a good idea,' I said.
'And when we've picked them, we can arrange them in some vases.'
'I'm good at that,' I said.
'Yes,' she said. 'You are.'

* * *

'Excuse me, sir.'

Kingston looked up. He had retreated into Holden's office once again. 'I need the privacy,' he had said publicly a couple of times, the second time in front of McPherson. But now he didn't bother to make an excuse and no one commented on it.

'Did you see my report on Bob Tapper?'

'I did indeed, Krystyna. A bit of a red herring, as I suspected it would be.'

'But he did have a history of violence, sir.'

'Sit down, Krystyna.' He gestured to the chair. 'Let's just take a look at the situation. He did have a history of beating his wife and at one point of stalking her, but none of that was recent. As you discovered, he lives within driving distance of Oxford, I admit. But much more significant was the fact that Bridget Moore told us very clearly that there had been no sign that he was still bothering her. She was convinced that if there had been, Julie would have mentioned it to her mother and her mother would have told Bridget. Or do you have a different memory of that conversation?'

'No, sir.'

'Anyway, he has a clear alibi — detained in High Wycombe station for several hours. You can't do better than that if you need a stay-out-of-jail-card for a more serious offence. It's just a shame that you didn't check that out sooner. It would have saved you a lot of time.'

'They had a computer problem. I rang to check it out and they apologized. They had noticed my interest in Tapper, and they rang in case this latest incident was relevant to us. They left a message with someone. But I never got it.'

'I know you meant well, and you tracked him down, so well done for that. We can put it down to experience.' He smiled a rather self-satisfied smile, one that underlined that he had been right all along and she was just an inexperienced young detective who had a lot to learn.

'Jim took the phone call. The guy at High Wycombe told me that,' she said.

'And Jim left a note about it on your desk. I am aware of that.'

'I never found it. In fact, I don't think he left any note. I think he is lying.'

Kingston sat up sharply. 'That's enough. You have made a very serious allegation against an experienced officer. In fact, the repercussions would be so serious for you that I shall pretend I never heard it. If you never saw the note, that must be because it got knocked onto the floor and the cleaners disposed of it. Do I make myself clear, Constable?'

'Yes, sir.'

'Now get back to your work.'

* * *

Andy Kingston loosened his tie. He wanted to take it right off, but he liked to think it gave him a bit of authority. Nowadays you often saw men in suits and shirts but no tie. Very 2020s. He envied the way they were able to carry it off, but somehow it didn't feel right to him. But now he was feeling uncomfortable in it and constricted too. And doubts over the case had started to creep in. He had Mullen in a cell, which was where he wanted him. McPherson had backed him in that, and yet the bastard had made it clear that if things didn't work out, if they weren't able to pin it on Mullen, then it would be his neck on the block. He stretched back in his chair, easing the dull ache in his back, and glanced around the office, catching sight of Frank Dickens making his way across the room. Dickens hardly ever came to the station

— he took pleasure in summoning them to his domain — so was this a good sign or a bad one?

Kingston was up on his feet in a flash, *bonhomie* personified. 'Frank! Nice to see you.'

'Got to pay a visit to my solicitor in the business park, so I thought I'd kill two birds, as it were.' He gestured toward Holden's cubicle. 'Maybe we could get a bit of privacy in there?'

Kingston followed him in and shut the door. He sat down, pulling at his collar. He was beginning to sweat.

'One or two things have come to light,' Dickens began. 'I'm afraid we've maybe been a bit slow off the mark.'

'What do you mean?' *Slow off the mark?* His words could only be the precursor to bad news.

'Miss Green. That's what we are calling the second victim. She deserves a name, don't you think? Anyway, to cut to the chase, Miss Green was pregnant.' A moment's pause. 'I imagine it might possibly be relevant to your investigation.' *You imagine!* How bloody long had he or someone in his team known this?

Kingston took a breath. 'How pregnant?'

'Five or six weeks.'

'I see.' Kingston's brain was beginning to crank into action, rather jerkily.

'I am led to understand that you are looking at the two cases being somehow connected, so I would also like to assure you that Julie Baxter was *not* pregnant.'

'Thank you.' Kingston didn't feel like thanking him, more like grabbing him by the scruff of the neck and asking him why the hell he hadn't reported this sooner.

'Do you have any information on Miss Green's identity yet?'

'Nothing much.'

'Nothing much?' Kingston's irritation levels were rising fast. 'You either have some information or you don't. Which is it?'

'I believe she has some Far Eastern blood in her, maybe Cambodia, Laos or Vietnam.'

'What the hell are you talking about?'

'Mixed parentage. Obviously she has taken after her European parent, but, well . . .' He dribbled to a stop. 'Anyway, as I said about the pregnancy, this may or may not be of help. But I hope it might.' He smiled with embarrassment, like a conjuror who has just messed up a not-very-difficult magic trick.

'How old was she?'

'Early twenties, I should think.'

'She was pregnant. Can you say if she was sexually experienced?'

'I would say so. And some of this experience may have been rather . . . rough.'

'You mean she'd been beaten up or raped? Julie Baxter had suffered that too, hadn't she?'

'There are significant differences.'

'In what sense?'

Dickens pursed his lips as he considered his reply. 'Julie Baxter had sustained broken bones that go back three or four years at least. And of course there was damage inflicted immediately prior to her death, but no sign of very recent sexual intercourse. In contrast, Miss Green has been hit recently, with damage to her ribs. She shows signs of having had sexual intercourse, also very recently, maybe within a day or two of her death.'

'Against her will?'

'The intercourse may have been quite, er, vigorous, but not necessarily against her will.'

'Any other surprises for me?'

'I am not sure if this is a surprise or not, but we've compared the dog hairs on Miss Green's coat and those you accessed from the dog called Rex, and they do seem a very good match.'

'What do you mean by "a good match?" Are they the same dog or not?'

'Very possibly. I can do more precise tests if you wish?'

'Yes, I do wish.'

'Very well.' Dickens got up out of his chair and turned to leave.

'Is there anything else?' Kingston snapped, his frustration now abundantly clear.

'I think that is about it.'

Kingston watched him leave. He was annoyed, yet the dog hairs surely proved that it was the same coat, and so surely the same woman. Once he had that information in black and white, Mullen's barrister would never be able to convince any jury that the woman in the pub and "Miss Green" were two different people. But in that case, why on earth had Mullen blurted out in front of the uniformed officers that he knew the dead woman. That didn't make sense — unless, of course, Mullen hadn't realized that the officers could hear him. He must have been talking to the Baines woman, unaware that they were right behind him. That would explain it. And once he had said it, he couldn't claim he hadn't.

Kingston walked out of Holden's office with a smile on his face. Things were coming together. And when the double case was all over and the dust had settled, maybe it would be his name affixed to Holden's door.

* * *

The Turf was quiet. It was eleven forty, so the lunchtime rush was yet to materialize. Becca ordered a mocktail. She needed a treat, but she had forsworn alcohol for as long as Doug was locked up. She hadn't told him, and she wouldn't either. It wasn't like she needed his thanks or approval. She could call it part of her new weight-loss regime, but that was only the half of it.

'Staying for lunch?' The guy on the other side of the bar had his hair pulled back and tied into a bun.

'I understand the police were here the other day.'

His eyes narrowed. 'What if they were?'

'Are you the manager?'

'I am today.'

She pulled a notebook out of her bag and opened it. 'The police were asking questions about a woman in a green coat and a man who met her here last week. I expect you might remember that.'

'Believe it or not, this place gets very busy.'

Becca looked around ostentatiously. A few students glued to their laptops, a group of three young Chinese women, an older woman and a young man, a middle-aged woman reading a book, an older man with a long beard and longer hair. 'Are any of these regulars?'

'Look, who are you exactly?'

'If I were to write a review about this place, I could be your worst nightmare.' She didn't wait for a response but got up and made a beeline for the bearded guy. It was either him or the woman engrossed in her book, but she hadn't looked up once. The chances were that a bomb could go off and she wouldn't notice.

In contrast, the guy had been observing her exchange with the man-bun. He was the sort of person she needed, sitting there drinking (very slowly) and watching what was going on. 'I wonder if you could help me.'

'That depends.'

'I'm looking to speak to someone who's a regular here.'

'You doing some sort of customer survey?'

'I guess you could call it that.'

He sniffed and looked down at his glass. It was three-quarters empty.

'I'll buy you a fresh one if you answer a few questions.'

He grunted and waved a hand at the man-bun, who gave a thumbs-up. 'Fire away, lady.'

'Were you here on Tuesday last week?'

'Very possibly.'

'About this time of day. There was a woman come in wearing a long, stylish green coat. Very shortly afterwards she was joined by a man with a small black dog. Do you remember them?'

He didn't answer immediately. Screwed up his face, looked over Becca's shoulder, nodded.

Man-bun appeared bearing a pint of beer and a card reader. She tapped her card and waited for him to deposit the beer and leave. She turned her gaze onto the bearded guy.

'Lie to me and that goes all down your shirt and trousers.'

He found that amusing. 'I'd like to see that, lady.'

Lady! She bit back her annoyance, and instead snapped out a question. 'What colour was her hair?'

'Grey, silver. That sort of thing. An elegant lady. I rather liked the look of her, actually.'

'Did you talk to her?'

'God, no. That's when things go wrong. You talk to someone and find they aren't what you expect.' He leaned forward conspiratorially. 'They always want something from you. Like you do.'

'She was wearing boots.' It was a test.

'Oh yes, very nice red ones.' Passed with flying colours. He looked around and pointed. 'She was sat over there, on that bench seat. She liked the dog. Let it sit on her while he got the drinks. It was a bit of a scrum that day. Someone's leaving do, I expect. Anyhow, the man sat on a little stool. He had orange juice or something poncy like that. She looked like she had a gin and tonic. Downed it pretty smartish too.'

Becca took a sip of her own "poncy" mocktail and told herself that however unpleasant, this man could well be her best bet. He had passed her test. He clearly remembered Kat.

'She wasn't that close to you, though, was she? I don't imagine you could hear anything they said.'

'I moved my table round a bit so I could get a proper look at her. You know what I mean.' There was a smirk on his face, and Becca suddenly felt ashamed to be sitting here encouraging this creepy man's creepy thoughts.

He finished his glass of beer in a long swig, then slipped his left hand round the one Becca had bought. He tapped at his head, just behind his ear, with the other hand. 'I had bad hearing until my cochlear implant. So I can lipread pretty well.' He winked at Becca. 'Makes sitting in a pub a bit more interesting.'

'So, were you able to work out anything that the woman in the green coat said?'

'Some.' He took a pull at his pint and lifted it in acknowledgement. 'Cheers, lady.'

She raised her own drink and took a sip. She wished now that she had ordered herself a double something.

'She said she could smell smoke in the dog's hair. Took a good sniff of it. Said something about feeling things. I reckon she was a bit . . . you know . . . not all there.'

'Really!' she said, mustering every ounce of the enthusiasm she didn't have.

'Then there was something else . . .' He took another swig of his beer. Hoping for another free pint, Becca reckoned, spinning things out.

'What was that?'

'The guy went back to the bar to get another round in. Coffees as it turned out. She was looking at her phone. Next thing was, she was speaking to someone and after that she stood up sharpish. She put the dog down on the seat, stroked his head, and then she left. Didn't wait for the coffee.'

'Any idea what she said on the phone?'

'That she was in the Turf. Then something about how she was having fun. She seemed rather edgy. She said "Sorry!" two or three times. That was about it.'

'Just "Sorry"?' Becca was beginning to think she was wasting her time. She hadn't learned anything new. And the guy had returned to his beer, taking two or three big gulps. 'Was that all?' she demanded, more sharply than she intended.

'What about another drink?' he said. 'It oils the memory.'

He stared at her, a challenge in his face. She stared back. She wasn't someone who easily backed down, and it was clear she had got out of him everything there was.

'Another day,' she said, and strode out of the pub.

* * *

94

Holden poured herself a glass of Chardonnay and settled down at her kitchen table with the sheaf of notes that Wozniak had surreptitiously printed out and removed from the office. Emails were too easily traced, and she would never get away with logging onto the network and accessing all the paperwork while she was on gardening leave and officially off the case. That would be all McPherson would need to get her permanently shifted to some shitty other job.

For some reason she found working through the evidence page by physical page — emails, pathology reports, Mullen's own evidence — to be more satisfactory than scrolling through digital documents. There were disadvantages, she knew, but somehow the information seemed to log itself in her brain much more easily when she saw it in black and white on paper.

The problem was that doing all this with an open bottle of wine did not lead to any blinding eureka moments. Rather the opposite. One small glass was followed by another small glass, and the more she read and the more she sipped, the less she seemed to understand. Instead, she found herself doubting her own judgement and questioning too her loyalty to Mullen. Maybe he had just flipped. Julie had turned down his advances at a time when his relationship with Becca Baines had run aground on the rocks of her trauma. He was stuck in a small house with her, sleeping on a sofa bed, frustrated. He wouldn't be the first man to kill because his sexual appetites had been denied. She poured herself another glass. Her eyelids were growing heavy, and she noticed with surprise that the bottle was now three-quarters empty.

There was also something bothering her, something she had read, and yet it was hidden in the fog of her brain. She would have to go to bed in a while and try again in the morning.

* * *

Holden woke up with a start. She had never made it upstairs to her bed, but instead had collapsed across the table. The bottle in front of her was now fully empty. The clock on the cooker told her it was just after six a.m. She pushed herself up onto her feet. Her mouth was dry and she had a low-grade headache at the back of her skull. She filled a glass with water and drank it down, followed by another. She switched on the kettle. She needed a cuppa and after that, a shower and then . . .

Her eyes focused on the fruit bowl sitting at the back of the kitchen worktop. How many times had she resolved to eat a healthier diet, and how many times had she ended up tossing rotten fruit into the bin? Right now, there were two wizened apples, a distressed pear and a single banana, whose mottled skin was more black than yellow. It was this particular piece of fruit on which her gaze was fixed. She frowned, trying to weigh and assess the thought that had entered her brain. She picked up the banana, as if touching it might aid the process. Slowly the tight lines on her face relaxed, and something approaching a smile appeared on it, unheralded. She peeled the skin back and — suddenly very hungry — bit into it, devouring it as if she had not eaten for week. Then she dropped the skin on the table, made her mug of tea and headed upstairs. She needed that shower.

* * *

'What the devil are you doing here?'

It was 8.05 a.m., and Detective Superintendent McPherson was glaring at the figure suddenly framed in his doorway. Susan Holden was wearing a bright red tracksuit, and her face was sticky with sweat and almost as red as her clothing.

'It's my new regime, going for an early morning jog. I was just coming through Florence Park when I thought to myself, why not call in on my good friend the detective superintendent?'

'This is totally inappropriate,' he spluttered.

'Is it OK if I sit down for a moment and catch my breath?' Without waiting for a reply, she shut the door behind her and settled herself on a chair opposite him.

'I want you to go home, Susan. Otherwise—'

'Otherwise what? You'll summon your goons to throw me out?' Holden's eyes were luminous in their intensity.

'If I have to summon security to have you removed from the building, then I will.'

'Ooh, I'm scared.'

'Have you been drinking?'

Instead of answering, she stood up and began to prowl around the room, nodding. 'I have a present for you,' she said. She dug her hand into her trouser pocket and tossed something at him with such suddenness that he squealed and ducked to avoid it. It caught him on the forehead and dropped limply onto his desk. He stared at the banana skin in amazement.

'Susan,' he said softly, 'I think you need to go and see your GP. You are in no state to be at work, and—'

'If you stand on one of those, you are in great danger of slipping up.'

'Susan?'

'I've come to warn you. For your own good. Before you make the most terrible mistake and—'

She never completed her sentence because the door burst open and two uniformed officers came in, immediately followed by two women. Holden stared at them, bemused.

'You're interrupting a meeting,' she said in her most imperious manner.

'Hello, Susan.' The woman who said this looked vaguely familiar. Grey hair tied back, blue eyes, heavily creased face. 'Remember me? I'm Jennie.' Her accent was Scottish, soft. Edinburgh rather than Glasgow.

'Have you come to see the detective superintendent? Well, let me tell you, I think he is making a huge mistake. That's why I have come here this morning, to protect him from himself. Do you understand?'

'I've come to see you, Susan,' the woman called Jennie said.

'Why?'

'I'd like you to put that down.' She pointed.

'What?'

'In your hand, Susan. Now please put it down on the desk.'

Holden wondered if the woman calling herself Jennie was all right. She glanced around the room. There was no way out. The two officers were standing in front of the door, which was shut, McPherson was on his feet behind his desk, and the other woman, the one with a hatchet face, had moved away from the others and was now positioned almost opposite Jennie. She was standing back against the wall, hands hanging down at her sides.

'Susan, I think you may have stopped taking your medication.'

Holden looked at Jennie again. Of course. Now she remembered. How could she forget?

'Susan, I am going to ask you one more time to put that knife down.'

Holden stared at her. What was the wretched woman talking about? She looked at her hand and saw to her amazement that she was holding something — a penknife — and that there was blood on her fingers. She squealed and dropped it, which galvanized the whole room into action. Before she knew it, the two officers had moved forward and taken a firm grip on her, and Jennie was saying, 'This is for your own good, Susan,' but it wasn't.

'Fuck you!' she screamed, and hurled herself forward in a desperate attempt to break free of their grip, but all that happened was that she found herself pinned to the floor and someone — the woman with the hatchet face, she guessed — was telling the men to damn well keep her still. She felt a stab of pain in her arm and yelled again. She made one last effort to break free, but when she tried to push herself up nothing happened. Someone was saying something to her that she didn't understand, and after that, everything passed into oblivion.

* * *

Becca ignored the blare of her mobile. She wasn't asleep despite the lateness of the hour. How late she didn't know, but it was dark and she had been trying ineffectually for what seemed like hours to make her thoughts slip into the place that unconsciousness brings. There was a short silence, and then it rang again. She forced herself to sit up. She'd have to answer it. Suppose it was the prison ringing. Suppose Doug had — God forbid — "done something" to himself. A tidal wave of panic suddenly swept through her, and she heaved her legs over the side of the bed and grabbed her mobile from the bedside cupboard.

'Yes?' she gasped into the phone. 'Becca Baines speaking'.

There was no answering voice, merely the sound of heavy breathing. 'Who is it?' she snapped, in a mixture of anger and fear. It was the middle of the night — 2.05 a.m. to be precise — so it could only be bad news.

'It's me. Detective Inspector Holden.' Her voice was low and slow, nothing like the woman Becca knew.

'Yes?' She didn't know what else to say, didn't want to ask the question that was on the tip of her tongue. She waited. But Holden didn't respond. Becca held the phone to her ear, listening to her breathing, until she could wait no more.

'Is everything all right, Susan?'

'I'm in the toilet.'

'What?'

'I'm in the toilet.'

'But is everything all right?'

'They've locked me in the hospital.'

'What do you mean?'

'They've got it all wrong.'

'Who have?'

'The police.'

'But you are the police.'

'They are trying to get rid of me.'

'Are they?'

'Because I am right and they are wrong.'

99

'Susan, it's the middle of the night. Perhaps I should come and talk to you tomorrow. Which hospital are you in?'

Holden didn't answer the question. Not that Becca had much doubt about it. Holden had clearly had some sort of mental breakdown, so she was very likely to be in the Warneford in Headington.

'The woman that Doug met in the pub, the one in the green coat. I need to know if she ate a banana while she was there.'

'A banana? Why?' Becca said.

'I can't tell you. Not over the phone. You don't know who might be listening. But it's a matter of life and death.'

And that was the last thing she said. Becca heard the gruff sound of a male voice in the background, and then a scream like that of a demon from hell, and then the phone went dead.

* * *

Becca bought herself a Campari and lemonade and went and sat down at a small table against the wall. Quite why she had opted for a drink she hadn't had for several years she didn't know, just that she needed something with a bit more kick than a fruit juice. Of course, alcohol did not fit in with her new healthy routine, but she had had her early morning walk with Rex, and now he was with her because he had, of course, been to the Turf before and had, according to Doug, behaved shamelessly well.

She had a good view of the comings and goings, but there was little enough of that this early, only a couple of tieless men in suits and two solitary individuals huddled over their laptops. The man she wanted to speak to, the man with the beard, was nowhere in sight. *Give it time*, she told herself. *Either he will come or he won't, and there's nothing you can do about it.*

So she took a couple of sips of her Campari, and absent-mindedly stroked the dog. She became so absorbed that she didn't realize the man had come in until his substantial shadow fell across the table.

'I remember you.' He pointed at her and winked. 'You're not stalking me are you, lady? Because that's a crime nowadays, I reckon.'

'Can I buy you a drink?' she said quickly, to which he, of course, replied in the affirmative.

A couple of minutes later, the man settled down opposite her with his drink in his hand and a smug expression on his face. 'So you've got more questions, have you? Or have you just taken a liking to me?'

'One question, actually.' She paused and took another sip of her drink.

'Fire away then.'

'It's about the woman in the green coat. This may seem like an odd question but it is important.'

He grinned. 'I'm all ears.'

'While she was here, did she eat anything?'

He made a face. 'Well, if you mean did they order any food, then the answer is no. She didn't stay long enough.'

'Anything else though? Crisps or nuts from the bar for example. Or something she brought with her in her handbag.'

'She didn't have a handbag. I'd have noticed if she had.' He lifted his beer and drank it down to the bottom. He belched. 'Beg your pardon. I'm right thirsty.'

Becca leaned forward. 'You haven't answered my question.'

He sniffed and sat back in his chair, appraising her. Then he uttered the words she had been hoping for but never expected. 'When the man got up to buy her a second drink, she pulled a banana out of her pocket and scoffed it down. Then another one. They weren't that big, mind you, but they disappeared fast enough. Then she got her mobile phone out and talked to someone, and the next thing was she was on her feet and heading for the exit.'

'So she left the banana skins on the table?'

'No. She stuffed them back into her pockets, surreptitiously, like she was worried in case the staff noticed. They don't like you eating your own food on the premises, do they?'

'I don't suppose they do.'

'But they love it if you're buying their beer.' And he pushed his glass across the table towards her.

* * *

Becca was barely out of the Turf before she sent a text to Holden. Then she headed for St Giles', where she had left her car, and drove home. There, she resisted temptation and ate a belated salad lunch. More than once she checked her mobile, in case Holden had responded, but eventually she gave up trying to be patient and rang her. Given that Holden had not responded to her text, she didn't in truth expect an answer, and she didn't get one. Perhaps she was expecting too much. How ill was Holden? To judge from some of the things she had said, she surely had a serious mental health problem. Why on earth had she rung in the middle of night and from a toilet? Because she didn't want to be overheard? Because she didn't want the staff to know she had a mobile phone? Or maybe it was because she was suffering from paranoia.

Becca would have been willing to bet money on paranoia if it had not been for one thing. The guy in the pub said he had witnessed Kat eating two bananas. She had herself been very careful to ask only if he had noticed her eating anything. It was he who had said bananas — two of them — which of course chimed exactly with Holden's question. So what exactly was the significance of these bananas to her?

She felt a wave of tiredness. She hadn't slept well, so she opted for forty winks and woke up an hour later suddenly alert.

Rex was whining. She looked around and saw he was at the door. There was a pleading look on his face. *Walkies, please?*

Didn't dogs ever get fed up with going for walks? That would be the sort of dog she would want, not one that dragged her out of the house morning, noon and night, come rain or shine. And a glance out the window was enough to confirm that this was going to be a case of rain. And more rain.

The two of them — woman and dog — headed for the old barn. Becca wasn't sure why. Since she had discovered the dead body, she had been wary of that route, but she couldn't discard the idea that maybe, just maybe, a visit to the crime scene might help her decide what to do next. It would also provide a brief shelter from the rain if it continued to chuck it down as it currently was.

The barn itself was now devoid of police tape, and of course there was no body, nor any obvious sign that anyone had been killed there. Just an old, little used barn that had long since seen better days.

She turned round and trudged back to the house, while Rex stopped and sniffed and then scuttled forward in front of her. The dog was, she realized, the only thing she could rely on in her life. What use was a police detective who was sympathetic but off her head? What use was Mullen to her in prison, even if he was innocent? She knew she shouldn't be thinking like that, but she wanted a baby and she wanted him to be the father.

She came to a halt some distance from her cottage. It was as if her feet were rooted to the ground, unable to advance a single step further. She knew what was happening, she was all too familiar with the nature of depression. She had thought she had got through it, but now, suddenly, she could feel it wrapping itself around her like a giant squid, engulfing its prey, and she didn't know how to cast it off.

She looked up, aware that the rain had eased to a drizzle and that the dog had disappeared. This shook her into life. She strode forward. If she let Mullen's pride and joy get run over or dog-napped, that would be the end. But suddenly he reappeared, barking with joy, twisting and jumping like the puppy he no longer was.

A figure appeared from behind the hedge, slim, well-groomed, blonde — everything that she herself wasn't. 'Are you Becca?' the woman said. 'I am Detective Constable Krystyna Wozniak, a colleague of DI Susan Holden.'

* * *

The two women sat in Becca's kitchen, facing each other across the table and cradling cups of tea. 'Susan is not very well,' Wozniak began.

'I know. She rang me in the middle of the night. From the toilet.'

'The toilet?'

'She seemed rather . . .' Becca paused, searching for the right word. 'Rather paranoid. Worried that someone might be listening.'

'She's been sectioned.'

'I thought as much.'

'The gossip round the station is that she has been seeing a therapist or psychiatrist for some time. She only returned to work a short while ago, but now . . .' Wozniak held out her hands. 'I am very worried for her.'

'When she rang—'

'From the toilet, you mean.'

'Yes. When she rang, she asked me to find out if the woman Doug met in the Turf had eaten a banana while she was there. I don't know why, but—'

'Ah,' Wozniak said, suddenly very alert. 'Of course.'

'What do you mean, of course?' Becca snapped.

'I'm sorry. What I mean is that I was one of the officers conducting Doug's second interview, and he mentioned that she had eaten a banana.'

'Actually, she ate two bananas.'

'Two?'

'I have spoken to a witness in the Turf who will testify to it, if that is necessary. But why is this important?'

'Because the dead woman that you found in your barn had an empty stomach and hadn't eaten for maybe twenty-four hours. But if the woman in the pub had eaten bananas at around noon the previous day, it proves that the woman in the pub and the dead woman were two separate people. Which is what your Doug insisted was the case.'

Becca put a hand to her mouth, her brain in a tailspin. She couldn't quite believe what Wozniak was saying, or what it meant.

'I need the details of the man you spoke to, Becca,' Wozniak continued. 'I will need to speak to him myself and get a formal statement, and then I will need to speak to my boss and then—'

'Doug will be set free?'

'It won't be my decision. But it seems to me that this new information seriously undermines the case against Doug.'

'I need to speak to his solicitor. Get her involved.'

'As you wish, Becca,' Wozniak said, but she lifted her hand in warning. 'If I may say so, I think the most important thing is that I first of all get a written statement from your source. Without that, we are no further forward.'

'Yes, of course.' Becca jumped up and grabbed her handbag from the peg on which it was hanging next to her damp coat. She rifled through it before triumphantly extracting a scruffy piece of paper. 'Here are his details.'

'Thank you.'

'One more thing. Alex — that is to say the man in the pub — told me that the woman put the banana skins back in her coat pocket. So I guess if you can find traces of banana in the dead woman's coat, it pretty much proves that both women wore the same coat, and that therefore there is a connection between the two.'

'Yes.' Wozniak sounded impressed. 'You would make a good detective yourself.'

But even as she said this, Wozniak's brain was tussling with another thought. Suppose there were no such banana traces in the coat, what then? That would work against Mullen. She looked at Becca, wondering if she had considered that possibility, but she had picked up the dog and was cuddling it with delight. Best not to point this out to her. Best just to carry on. She would ring Dickens and see if he could check the pockets for residue. Get a written statement from this Alex. Then present her findings to Kingston and see how he reacted.

CHAPTER 8

As for Ngung, it wasn't just the pregnancy that forced me to act. It was letting Kat escape. Or rather, not just letting her, but helping her. One of my rules — my strictest rule — was that both of them should remain inside the confines of the house and grounds. 'For your safety!' I told them both. Kat for obvious reasons: she wasn't capable of getting around safely. But Ngung because she was an illegal. She had no papers, no passport, no money. I sent money to her family back in Vietnam as I promised. Not a fortune, admittedly, but she would have had a much worse life back there.

But once she was pregnant, she changed. She became cocky, full of herself.

'I thought it would be a treat for her,' Ngung told me when I challenged her. 'She said she wanted to meet a friend at the Turf Tavern. I think that is nice for her.'

'The friend was a man,' I snapped back at her.

But all she did was shrug in a rather insolent manner. 'I not know that.'

She even helped her hire a taxi. She thought I was away, busy at a meeting in one of the colleges, and that I would never find out. But the meeting didn't last long because the keynote speaker was involved in a car accident that morning, so I came back home and discovered that Kat wasn't there.

And then the man she met turned out to be a private eye. Doug Mullen for crying out loud!

The problem is that I had no idea what she said to the guy. Was she in any state to tell him anything incriminating? Half the time she is out of it — the power of medication — but she managed to get to the Turf, so I couldn't be sure. And why did she want to meet him anyway? Had someone put her up to it?

My first thought was that it must have been Ngung, but I didn't see how she would have come up with the idea of approaching a private investigator. But later, when I thought about Julie and saw how much Kat liked her and how fond Julie seemed to be of her, I had this sudden revelation that perhaps it had been her who put Kat up to it. Not that it matters now.

* * *

The atmosphere in the room was anything but cordial. McPherson himself had descended from his office on the floor above "just to sit in." But if his words were meant to make Andy Kingston feel relaxed and supported, they failed miserably. He felt as if he were on trial, and he also felt as if the case was in danger of disintegrating in his hands. He had misread Krystyna. He had been distracted by her physical attractiveness, and that had blinded him to the fact that she was a clever and ambitious detective constable who was clearly set on making a name for herself.

'So, you lead, Andy. You can think of me as a fly on the wall.'

Kingston took a sip of water. He wished McPherson really was a fly on the wall. Then he'd be able to squash him with the flat of his hand.

'Thank you, sir. Well, the fact is we have come up with some evidence that may shed new light on the case.'

McPherson said nothing, but his lips twitched. He didn't look the slightest bit happy.

'Particular credit must go to Krystyna,' Kingston said. He had decided that rather than isolate her on the fringes of the investigation — as he had been trying to do — he needed

107

to emphasize that she was a valued, fully integrated member of the team. But first he wanted to make it clear that she was fallible. 'She first investigated Julie's Baxter's ex, Bob Tapper, who lives not so far away in High Wycombe. Her suspicions that Tapper could have killed Julie were well-founded, but Jim did some checking on the system and discovered that on the night in question, Tapper had spent several hours in High Wycombe police station following an incident outside a pub in the city centre.'

'So a dead end,' McPherson said bluntly.

Wozniak clenched her teeth. *Jim did some checking!* That was manipulation of the truth. She wanted to protest, but knew it would get her nowhere.

'That's often the way, sir,' Kingston said, pressing quickly onwards. 'But other leads have been more positive.'

'Thank God for that!' For a fly on the wall, McPherson was making a lot of noise.

'We noticed something odd. We would have spotted it sooner if Dickens hadn't been rather slow in keeping us informed.' He paused. He had no compunction in smearing Dickens with a bit of blame. 'He told us rather belatedly that the second victim, whom we are calling Miss Green, was pregnant. To be fair, he did apologize, but even so that delay was unhelpful for the investigation.' He raised his hands in apparent frustration. 'Anyway, we also learned another important thing from him, namely that Miss Green had not eaten for a long time before her death. Again, credit to Krystyna, she noticed a discrepancy, namely that according to Mullen's testimony, the woman he met in the pub had eaten a banana while she was there.' He paused, allowing Wozniak her bit of praise. But he had no intention of making it appear that it was a one-woman show. 'Obviously, we only had Mullen's word for this, so we followed it up, and the result was that we identified a reliable witness in the pub, who stated that on the day in question he saw the woman eat not one, but two bananas. That, of course, throws a new light on things and—'

McPherson swore. 'So what you're saying is that Mullen was telling the truth, that there were two different women and that he, Mullen, is not the killer.'

'Mullen is still most definitely a suspect. There is some forensic evidence, indeed some blood, that places him at the scene of the second crime.'

'But not the first. The key question is this: do you have enough evidence to continue to hold him?'

Kingston said nothing. It was as if his tongue had tied itself in a knot.

'Let me spell it out for you, Andy, and indeed for every-one in this room. Your case is looking precarious. You're not going to convince a jury on the strength of the evidence you've got. You need to gather more, and you need to gather it fast. And may I point out that as I understand it, you know virtually nothing about this "Miss Green" except that she was pregnant, and nothing about the woman who met Mullen in the pub — except that she likes eating bananas!'

'That's not quite true, sir,' Kingston said, but without conviction. He glanced around the room, hoping to elicit support from his team, but nearly all of them seemed to have spotted something on the floor that demanded their undivided attention. Only Wozniak came to his aid.

'The woman in the Turf called herself Kat with a "K,"' she said firmly. 'She attended one of the Oxford colleges when she was a young woman. Of course, that doesn't nar-row down the field too much, since we can only guess at her age, but I am confident that with a bit of work we can narrow it down a lot further.'

'Confident, are you, Constable? With the benefit of all your experience, you think you can solve the case.'

Wozniak ignored the sarcasm. 'I see no reason why, working as a team, we cannot identify her.'

McPherson glared at her. She held his gaze. Her mother had taught her to stand up for herself, and she had learned the lesson well.

'We'll see.' McPherson turned back towards Kingston. 'You've got until the end of the week to come up with more evidence. Otherwise it's a case of releasing Mullen. So for crying out loud, make some progress. I've got the commissioner breathing down my neck, so if we do release Mullen there's going to be shit flying all over the place and, Andy, most of it will end up deposited on your desk. Do I make myself clear?'

* * *

'Have you got a minute, sir?'

Kingston looked up and scowled at Wozniak. 'Well, what is it? It had better be important.'

'You can be the judge of that, sir.'

'Spit it out then.'

'Earlier this morning, I was on the phone with Julie Baxter's mother, Marjorie. She's very distressed.'

'I can't do anything about that.'

'I know, sir. It's just that she asked about Julie's diary. She is keen to get it back when we have finished with it.'

'It's evidence.'

'I did say that to her, sir.'

'So that's all right then.'

'Who's dealing with it, sir? In view of the chief super's comments, I wondered if maybe we should see if it gives us any new angles on the case. I mean, without wishing to rock the boat, I wonder if perhaps we should consider the possibility that Mullen isn't guilty.'

She stood still, wondering how he would react. He had already savaged her over Royce and the missing note he said he had left on her desk.

'I'm probably jumping up the wrong tree . . .' she continued.

To her surprise, Kingston smiled. 'Barking, Krystyna. It's barking up the wrong tree.'

'Oh, sorry.'

'Take a look at the diary. Discreetly, mind you. I don't want the rest of the team getting distracted. Nothing on the computer system. Handwritten notes. If you have anything to report, then speak directly to me only. Do you understand?'

'Yes, sir.'

'Go through it but keep an open mind. And don't ignore Mullen. See if you can spot anything that links her to him. Maybe she used to cut his hair.' Kingston grinned, pleased with himself. 'Mind you, he looks to me like a man who opts for a number one cut in the local barbers.'

'Yes, sir.'

'Or has Mullen lived near any of the addresses in Julie's diary?' His voice was hard again. 'She could have met him that way, had an affair that turned out messy. If there is any link like that, I want to know pronto.'

'Absolutely.'

'But remember, I don't want this to interfere with your other duties, Krystyna.'

'No, sir.' She turned away, disconcerted by the way his gaze lingered on her. She was conscious that he had started to look at her in much the same way as men in the street, men who had never met her. They often looked at her, appraising her, their eyes sweeping up and down. She wished Susan Holden was back in charge.

* * *

It was late afternoon. Outside, the rush hour was in full swing as cars, vans and buses crawled along the Oxford Road past the police station and out towards the ring road. The office had thinned out. Kingston and Royce had not returned from whatever it was they had been doing. Wozniak was steadily getting on top of all the tasks that had been dumped on her, and now that there was no one around to monitor her, she took the opportunity to devote a few minutes to Julie Baxter's diary.

On the outside it was a bog-standard A5 diary of the type you can buy at any high-street stationers: red, the year emblazoned in mock gold, and inside a week spread over two pages. Every hair-dressing appointment was recorded in immaculately neat writing: time, full name, a postcode, fee charged and a tick indicating payment, with either a "c" or "£" next to it, which she quickly assumed referred to card or cash payment.

At the back, the several lined pages headed *Notes* contained the full name and address details of her clients. In a couple of places, a red line had been drawn neatly through the name, indicating they had ceased to be her customer for one reason or another.

So far, so good. But what to do with all this information?

* * *

'So, how are things down at the station?'

The man asking the question was well over six feet tall and solidly built, with a face — especially the nose and ears — that harked back to his university rugby days. He had narrowly missed winning a blue for the Oxford University rugby team, and in his first year as an undergraduate, he had played for the Greyhounds (the second fifteen). In his second year he had appeared a nailed-on certainty for a blue until he dislocated a shoulder a week before the match. He failed to return to college the following term, for reasons that he never discussed. No one in their right mind ever asked him why.

'Busy,' was the reply.

'You're in the middle of a double murder case. Of course you're busy.'

Jim Royce shrugged. 'McP is getting his knickers in a twist.'

'Nothing new in that.' He laughed. 'Anyway, you've got your man, all you need to do is nail him down in court.'

Royce didn't reply immediately. He wasn't sure how much to say — or not to say. In the end, he took another pull at his beer and then leaned forward so he could drop his voice to a whisper.

'Problem is the evidence has gone a bit shaky.'

'What? You mean you've got the wrong man?'

'No. But McP has decided the evidence isn't sufficient. Dickens came into the station in person and threw a spanner in the works, and that has got him all on edge.'

'But you haven't released this Mullen guy, have you? I've not heard about it.'

'We've got two or three days to sort things out or he goes free.'

'So find the evidence.'

'That's what McP said.'

The man with the rugby nose emptied his glass and slapped it down on the table. 'Then one way or another, you need to find some evidence. And if you have to break a few rules to get it, then that's what you have to do. Working on a case that goes tits up isn't going to speed your ascent up the promotion ladder, is it?'

'I know.'

The man stood up and pulled on his black coat, carefully buttoning it up. Tailored, a sign of the man's wealth. 'Just keep me informed.'

'Sure.'

He turned to go, but then appeared to change his mind. 'How is your young lady?' he said. 'I should have asked earlier.' But he didn't wait for an answer. Instead, he pulled an envelope out of his pocket and placed it carefully in front of Royce. 'Treat her to a nice holiday when this case is over.'

Royce didn't thank him, merely pulled the envelope off the table and out of sight. 'And how are things with you?'

The man gave a thin smile. '*Plus ça change*, Jim. *Plus ça change*.'

* * *

They met outside the Limoncello in Abingdon. It was a small, discreet Italian restaurant, which suited both of them

— Becca Baines because she didn't much fancy the drive into Oxford, and Krystyna Wozniak because she wanted to avoid anywhere she might bump into her police colleagues.

Becca was early so she decided to wait outside for a few minutes, and before she had finished checking her mobile phone, there Krystyna was. She gave Becca a hug, which took her by surprise, but she found herself hugging back almost desperately, craving the physical comfort of someone's arms around her.

'Becca, we are friends, yes?' Krystyna said quietly into her ear. 'We must look like friends, just in case.'

'Yes.'

'Even though I am police.'

'I understand.'

Inside, tucked away out of the view of passers-by, they both opted for a spritzer and a vegetarian lasagne.

'I will pay,' Becca said firmly.

'You have cash?'

She nodded.

'Then that is OK.'

Throughout the meal they chatted as friends. Becca could sense the careful probing behind Krystyna's questions, but they didn't feel intrusive, and she felt she could be open, about her past, her living arrangements, and even — perhaps especially — about the baby. When she found herself gently weeping over her empty plate, it was Krystyna who waved the waiter away, buying her time to recover, and then briskly ordered two cappuccinos when another waiter came to see if everything was "satisfactory."

'Becca,' she said, when the coffees had been delivered and the storm of grief had abated, 'I think you should know that I am being, how shall I say, sidelined.'

'Sidelined? Are you sure?'

'They give me jobs that no one else wants.'

'Perhaps that's because you are new to the team?'

'You think that is OK? When I am smart.'

'No,' Becca replied quickly. 'I am playing devil's advocate. Perhaps you are too smart for them. They feel threatened.'

'I get given the job of tracking down Julie's ex-husband. DS Kingston thinks this is a waste of resources, so he gives it to me. I track down his mother. I track him down. I find he lives in Slough, not so far from Oxford. He is a nasty man, like his mother. But it turns out he got into a fight in High Wycombe that night and was held for questioning overnight while he sobered up.'

'Shouldn't that have been on police records?'

'There were computer problems in High Wycombe. But someone rang our office and spoke to Jim Royce, and he claims he left a note on my desk, but I never saw it. He lied. They are trying to "take me down a peg," my brother says. I think they are bastards.'

'You said you were smart.'

'Smarter than Royce, that is for sure.'

'Maybe that is why you are unpopular. Maybe you need to concentrate on being less smart. If you see what I mean?'

Wozniak frowned. 'No, I not see.'

'They think you are big-headed. They will not like that.'

'Ah!' There was a dawning of self-recognition in Wozniak. But it was only partial. 'I do not agree with them. Also I like Susan.'

'Like her?'

'I think she is better than all of them, and I trust her judgement about Doug, and I hate them for driving her to the edge of craziness.'

'Do they still think Doug is a murderer?'

'Yes. They are keeping me in the office, doing all the dogsbody work, while they try and construct a strong-enough case to convince the crime prosecution service to prosecute Doug. So I have come here to ask for your help.'

'In what way?'

She pushed a white envelope across the table. 'Put this in your bag. You must keep it safe and return it to me later.

It contains the diary belonging to the woman your Doug spoke to in the cinema — Julie Baxter. She was a hairdresser, visiting people in their houses. No one has followed this up because they don't think it can possibly be relevant to Doug. But if Doug is not the killer, as we both believe, then this diary might lead us to Kat, and if we find Kat, maybe we find the killer.'

'So, you want me to visit Julie's clients?'

'I asked my sergeant if I can do this but he still thinks the killer is Doug. So he says I can look into these people in Julie's diary, but it is not a priority. And he also gives me lots of other work, which makes it difficult for me and keeps me in the office.'

'I'll do it. Of course I will.'

Wozniak leaned even closer to Becca. 'Be careful. If you find Kat, you might be in danger. This is no game.'

Krystyna's phone beeped. She looked at it, frowned and thrust it into her pocket. 'I will have to go.' She stood up and gesticulated towards the waiter who went scurrying off to retrieve her coat. She was a woman who could turn men into putty. 'I am relying on you, Becca, and so is Doug. You can do things that I cannot.'

Then the waiter was back, unnecessarily helping her with her coat. She gave him a curt nod and slipped something into his hand. A tip, Becca assumed, but when she summoned the waiter a few minutes later to ask for the bill, she was told, 'Your charming friend has already paid.'

* * *

Becca had come up with a plan. Visit all the relevant clients in Julia's diary — Katherines, Cathys, Kates and so on — and explain that Julia was no longer able to do their hair. Ask if they would like her to take Julie's place. Somewhere in the midst of this, she hoped to identify the woman in the Turf who liked to call herself Kat, who had once been at university in Oxford. She was — what had Doug called her? — "a little bit doolally." When you added it all up, it gave her something to be going on with.

The question was where to start. At the very beginning maybe, as Julie Andrews sang in *The Sound of Music*. Start with January then. There was a Katerina and a Catherine in the first two weeks she looked at. They certainly fitted the bill. And a Kathy in the next week. Those would do as starters.

But it began badly. It took her over half an hour to get to Katerina Westacott in Oxford's Summertown, and two minutes of ringing the bell fruitlessly to realize that either the woman wasn't at home, or she was at home but, for some reason or another, had no intention of answering the door. Short of breaking and entering there wasn't much else she could do except push a handwritten note through the door — which she did.

The next client, Catherine Mead, lived a short drive away, in Cutteslowe. Becca pulled up in Templar Road, ignoring the fact that she was parking in a residents' only spot. She also ignored the *No cold callers* sign and pressed the bell. She saw movement through the frosted glass pane in the door and gathered herself. For of course she was a cold caller, with (like all cold callers) a prepared spiel all ready to be released on the unsuspecting resident as soon as she opened the door.

When the door did open, it was only by a small amount. An elderly woman's face appeared.

'Who are you?'

'My name is Becca—'

'Go away. Can't you read?'

'I'm a friend of Julie, your hairdresser.'

'She's dead.'

'Oh, you know.'

'I do read. Just because I'm old, that doesn't mean I'm daft. It's been all over the *Oxford Mail*, not to mention BBC Oxford.'

'Is there any chance that I could use your toilet?'

'Oldest trick in the book.'

'Please.'

The woman frowned, shut the door. There was the rattle of a security chain being released and then the door opened again, this time wide. 'You pregnant? My wife used to pee a lot when she was pregnant.'

Becca was stunned. Those two words, "you pregnant?" made her gasp with pain. It felt like she had been kicked in the stomach. 'No,' she said. 'No.' But she couldn't stop the tears from welling up in her eyes.

'After you've been to the toilet, how about a cup of tea?' Catherine Mead said. 'If you've got time, that is.'

When Becca had recovered herself, she went through to the kitchen, where Catherine was making tea in two mugs. She had pulled her wig off and was scratching at her scalp.

'Julie was brilliant,' she said quietly. 'When my beloved died, I decided I wanted to live as a woman, and Julie was so supportive. She used to shave my head and oil it and listen to me rabbit on and make suggestions about what I should wear — and what I should not wear!' She laughed at the memory.

'I suppose Julie never talked about her other customers, did she?'

'I'm afraid not, sweetie. She refused to gossip about them. Which was a shame because the wife and I loved a bit of a gossip.'

'I'm interested in just one of them. She called herself Kat. Kat with a "K." I'm not sure if that was made up or what.'

'I still can't help you. I wish I could. But maybe there's something else you'd like to talk about? I'm a good listener.'

So Becca talked. Catherine indeed was a good listener, and by the time Becca drank the final cold remains of her tea and checked her watch, she was amazed at how long she had been there. 'You've been really kind,' she said as she left. Catherine, her wig now firmly back in place, stood in the doorway and waved. Becca waved back. *She's lonely*, she reflected, as she turned the car round and headed back towards the Banbury Road. *She's lost a wife and is now trying to identify as a woman.* Becca wasn't sure she could truthfully imagine what that might be like, but Catherine must, surely, be lonely. Becca was so preoccupied with these ruminations that she never noticed a silver BMW slip out of its parking place and follow at a distance. Perhaps if she had, things might have gone very differently.

* * *

Catherine Mead didn't mind going out in the evening. The fact was that she felt more comfortable doing so then than in the daytime. She got fewer funny looks in the dark. The woman who had called earlier had been so kind that she had decided to treat herself to a nice Chinese meal. She could have ordered one and got it delivered, but it was ridiculous to pay the extra when she was quite capable of walking down to the takeaway. Money didn't grow on trees after all, and she needed to be braver. After all, she wouldn't have thought twice about it before.

But that was *before*. Now, *after*, the fact was that things were different. She had ordered over the phone — spring rolls and chicken chow mein — so that she wouldn't have to hang around. All she would have to do was pay and go. As she walked, she thought about Becca Baines and the reason she had come to her door. It had been a bit like being part of one of those crime dramas she loved to watch on TV. She wished she could have helped her.

Back home, with the food on the table and a glass of beer to go with it, she felt a glow of happiness. She began to eat and wondered if maybe Becca would return. She had left her scarf behind. What would Freud have said about that — did she subconsciously want an excuse to come back? She hadn't left any contact details, so she couldn't ring her and tell her. Catherine finished the second of her three spring rolls and followed it with a sip of beer.

She was about to sip again when the doorbell rang. Who on earth? It must be Becca, back for her scarf. Catherine got up and went to the door. She slipped the chain and swung the door wide open in welcome — and immediately regretted it.

'Thames Valley Police,' the man said. He was a big man, short-haired, in a dark suit and white shirt.

'Have you got ID?'

'No need for that, this is an unofficial visit.'

Catherine tried to shut the door, but the man's foot was in the way, and he pushed himself in. 'Nice smell. Chinese, if I'm not mistaken.'

'I'm eating my supper. I'd like you to leave.'

'I'll leave when you've answered my questions.'

Catherine flinched as the man brushed past her. For a moment she considered running out of the front door and down the road, but she still had her high heels on, so she resigned herself to answering the questions.

'A woman came to see you earlier today. I must warn you that she is a very cunning con artist, so it is important that you tell me what she said and what you told her, so we can protect you and others. We'll start with an easy question. What was her name — or perhaps I should say what did she call herself, because it probably wasn't her real name?' The man stretched out a hand and picked up the uneaten spring roll. 'I'm starving,' he said, and ate it in two bites.

'Becca,' she whispered.

'Spot on. By the way, that was a test. We know the name she operates under. If you had lied, that wouldn't have been a good start.'

Catherine nodded. Fear had begun to seep into her bones.

'So what did she ask you about?'

She took a deep breath as she tried to decide how to play this. What would be safest? 'It was about my hairdresser, Julie. She asked me if I knew that Julie had died and she wondered if I would like her to be my hairdresser from now on. So I said I'd think about it.'

'You're not telling me porkies, are you? Because if I'm not very much mistaken, that is a wig on your head.'

Catherine paused, then pulled it off. 'Julie shaves my head when she comes. Rubs oils into it. She first started to come to the house when my wife was taken ill. We got pally with her and when she died and I decided to transition, I asked her if she'd mind coming back and looking after me.'

The man didn't say anything, but there was a look of distaste on his face. He sniffed. Then he stood up, pulled some blue plastic gloves from his pockets and began to put them on. 'You must think I was born yesterday,' he said.

'What do you mean?' Catherine began to panic. 'It's exactly as I said. I'm not lying. Honestly!'

'Why you? Why did she come to you?'

'Because I was one of Julie's clients.'

The man's face curled up into a snarl. His whole body shuddered. Then he moved with surprising deftness across the short distance to Catherine, grabbed her with one hand and hit her hard with the fist of his other.

'I said, why *you*?'

'Because, because, because of my name.' She was weeping with terror and pain.

'That's better,' he said. 'That wasn't so difficult, was it? Now I've just got a couple more questions. And all you've got to do is answer them truthfully.'

She nodded frantically, conscious that she had wet herself, and conscious too that whoever this guy was, he was not a policeman.

CHAPTER 9

'Bloody hell!'

Andy Kingston was standing in the living room doorway, Jim Royce at his shoulder, surveying the scene in front of him. The CSI team were already there, with Dickens fussing around, instructing the two detectives to stand in one particular place. The room itself was largely undisturbed. There was a half-eaten meal — Chinese to judge from the smell of it — on the table. A glass was lying on its side, and from it a brown liquid had drained across the table and down onto the pale carpet. There was a Newcastle Brown ale can lying on its side in front of the unlit gas fire. The other object of interest, a couple of feet away from the can, was a wig. The words "cancer" and "chemotherapy" jumped into the forefront of Kingston's mind. He had seen his mother travel along that road until morphine and death took her to a place without pain. He felt a sudden urge to be anywhere but in this house and in this front room.

After the wig, Kingston's attention inevitably returned to the dead woman. She was lying on her back, arms akimbo, legs splayed. Her pink flowery dress was crumpled but unmarked. A see-through polythene bag had been pulled over her head, the sort of thing Kingston and his wife used when freezing vegetables and fruit from his allotment.

'What do you think, guv?' Royce seemed to find his boss's silence unnerving, but Kingston ignored him. He doubted that the woman had died of asphyxiation, because there was a heck of a lot of blood inside the bag, which suggested a pumping heart while she was being smashed about the head. There were only a couple of trails of blood showing on her neck, so if the intention had been to limit the mess and the chance of the killer being covered in blood while he — surely this had to be the work of a man — battered the woman to death, it had been almost wholly successful.

Kingston tried to ignore the nausea rising in his gullet. 'Who is it?'

'I understand they identify as Catherine Mead,' Dickens said.

Kingston was momentarily puzzled. 'Identify?'

'I expect you might call her a man. He was transitioning, so I think we should respect that and call her she or they.'

'I'm not here for a lecture,' Kingston snapped. 'But time and manner of death would be useful.'

'Last night, mid-evening maybe. I suggest you check with the local Chinese and see when she picked her takeaway up. In my experience, people who buy takeaways like to eat them pretty much immediately, and of course she never finished hers, so—'

'Thank you, Sherlock. I don't suppose that line of reasoning would have occurred to either myself or my colleague.'

'All part of the service.' Dickens was rather enjoying getting under Kingston's skin.

'Any sign of it being a hate crime?' Kingston paused. 'Any *obvious* signs, I mean.'

As he faced the two detectives, Dickens felt his good humour evaporate. His back was aching and the thing he most wanted was for them to clear off and let him get on with his crime scene. 'If you're asking if anyone has cut off the testicles or penis, the answer is no. But someone has smashed her head in pretty comprehensively, even though the bag would have killed her pretty efficiently without any such violence. I would imagine that implies a considerable degree of dislike. Whether there was something personal in that, or whether the killer merely had an aversion to men who dress up as women, I'll let you decide.'

'So she didn't suffocate as such?'

'A combination of suffocation and violent assault, I would say. The result was the same.'

'Who rang it in?'

'The postie, I believe.'

'Right, we'll speak to him and let you get on with it.'

Dickens smiled smugly. 'I think you'll find the postie is a her, not a him.'

The two detectives stared back at him with such loathing that he shivered involuntarily.

'Well, don't let us delay you,' Kingston said.

The young one, Royce, the one who had fallen on Julie Baxter's body, said nothing. But if looks could kill, Dickens reckoned that he himself would at this very moment have been toppling over backwards, a bullet hole in the middle of his forehead.

* * *

Becca wouldn't have found two uniformed police hanging around outside her house if she hadn't parked so incautiously in Cutteslowe's Templar Road the day before. When she went to call on Catherine Mead, she had pulled up immediately opposite the home of Mrs Rose Ramsden. This woman was well known locally as a demon curtain twitcher, so, when the police had come calling during their house-to-house enquiries the next day, it was as if all her birthdays had come at once.

'Honestly, people like her. You wouldn't credit it, would you? She just abandoned her car half on the pavement and half off. Not a thought in her head about how inconvenient it was for the likes of me.'

The police officer nodded and asked if she could give him any more details.

'Of course I can,' she said triumphantly. 'I believe in backing up my complaints with evidence. Otherwise they never do anything about it, do they — the council or indeed you police if you don't mind me saying so. But I do understand that you have more important matters in the areas of public safety and crime prevention to worry about, so please don't take it personally.'

Jake Railton nodded again and smiled widely to indicate that he had no intention of taking her jibe personally. 'You mentioned having some evidence?'

'Look, Officer, this here is a residents' parking area, so it is an actual offence, not just an inconvenience, when people park their vehicles here without permission and indeed without any mitigating reason. Anyway, this woman got out of the car. Red it was. She was in her mid-thirties I'd guess, and she was also what my Ted would have called "well-up-holstered." Anyway, when she went inside Number Twenty-seven, I realized she wasn't just a delivery person dropping off a package but that she was here to stay. So I waited five minutes just in case I had misjudged her, and then I took action. I may look like a daft old woman, but there are no bats in my belfry. You see, my son gave me this mobile phone at Christmas, which was very kind of him. Mind you, he could just as easily ring me on my home phone, but he worries about me, bless him. Anyway, the best thing about this mobile phone is that it takes photographs, so that's what I use it for mostly. It's my contribution towards keeping the community safe.'

She paused to regain her breath, and Railton nodded yet again, wondering if this rambling would eventually lead to something productive.

'Anyway, just give me a minute.' Rose Ramsden was busy fiddling with her phone, and after several grunts of frustration she triumphantly looked up at the officer. 'Here you are! I took these. Quite good if I say so myself. This one here is the car, and so is this one. Not much difference, I admit, but you can see the number plate very clearly in both. And this one is much later, when she finally came out of Number Twenty-seven. I nearly missed it because I had to go to the toilet, but I reckon you will be able to tell who the woman is.'

'Fantastic!' The officer was grinning with pleasure. 'Thank goodness there are people like you in Oxford helping us overworked police catch the law-breakers on our streets. Might I borrow your phone for a day or two until we have finished assessing the evidence of your photos? I'll make sure it is returned to you.'

'Of course,' she said. 'Anything to help the Old Bill.' And she laughed, delighted that he had taken her seriously. She watched him go across the road to talk to another officer. That had to be a good sign. She thought she would write to Thames Valley Police and congratulate them on the calibre of their young officers. She was sure they would be encouraged to receive a nice letter rather than all the criticism that you often saw in the newspapers and on the BBC news.

Becca was — of course — oblivious to all this. It was late afternoon, and she was returning from a long walk with Rex, when she saw the police car pull up outside her house. Anxiety rippled through her. A visit from the police never seemed to bring good news.

'Ms Becca Baines?' the female officer said as soon as she was within speaking distance.

She nodded cautiously, wondering what had happened.

'I wonder if you would mind accompanying us to the Cowley Road police station?'

'What the hell for?'

'My colleagues have some questions that they wish to put to you. It would be most helpful if you could come with us now.'

'I was going to make myself some tea. I've not eaten in ages. And what about my dog?'

'Leave him in the house with food and water. We'll drive you home afterwards.'

* * *

126

McPherson watched the interview leaning back in a chair, his eyes half closed. Despite appearances he was fully alert. It was Kingston and Royce again. Wozniak had been sidelined back to her desk — a fact that hadn't escaped McPherson's notice. She was junior and inexperienced, of course, but he had no doubt that she would go further than both these two if she played her cards right.

Althea Potter was sitting next to Baines, a calm and mostly silent presence, yet alert to all the tricks of the trade. She watched and listened as the two men tried to get under the skin of an edgy Baines, at one point placing her hand very firmly on her client's lower arm as she had previously done to Mullen. But whereas he had accepted it for the warning it was, Baines had flinched visibly and pulled her arm away.

'So, let me just get this clear,' Kingston was saying. 'You visited Catherine Mead because you thought she might be the person Doug Mullen claims to have met in the Turf Tavern. Why her?'

'Because she was one of Julie's clients. Initially it was the wife who was the client, but after a while, when Catherine decided to identify as a woman, Julie took her on too.'

'And how did you discover that she was one of Julie's clients?'

Baines didn't answer immediately. McPherson noticed this. There was a definite pause. Then Baines said, 'Julie's mother told me.'

Did she really? McPherson's suspicions were aroused.

'You mean you went round to her house and spoke to her?' Kingston said. 'You shouldn't have done that. You should have left it to us.'

'You've arrested a friend of mine who I know for a fact is an innocent man. Why on earth would I rely on you to do anything?'

'My client is tired,' Potter said sharply. 'She is cooperating fully with your enquiries. If you have any other questions to ask, now is your opportunity. Otherwise I must insist you either charge her or let her go home.'

Kingston pointedly ignored Potter. He stared fixedly at Baines. 'Ms Baines, the fact is that Catherine Mead is now dead. Which seems to me to be very convenient for your boyfriend—'

'Lodger,' Potter snapped. 'Mr Mullen is and has been my client's lodger ever since his own home was burned down in a violent act of arson.'

'He sounds like more of a friend than a lodger to me, but the crux of the matter is that now that Mead is dead, Mr Mullen can claim that it was her he met at the Turf, and there is no one alive to deny it.'

'It wasn't Catherine Mead that Doug met at the pub,' Baines said wearily. 'I am convinced of it.'

'What makes you say that?'

'Observation and intuition.'

'Perhaps you can explain what you mean.'

Potter ostentatiously started to tidy up her paperwork. 'My client will make no further comment on this line of questioning.'

'That is a shame, especially as I understood she was keen to cooperate with us.'

'Tell me, Sergeant,' Potter said, clipping her briefcase shut, 'do you have forensic evidence that gives a time of death for Mead? It's just that I could not help noticing that you have not said anything about that. My client has stated openly when it was that she called on Mead and approximately how long she was there. Do the forensics on the dead body indicate that she died at that time of day? Or do they point to a time much later in the day, or even during the night?'

McPherson's half-closed eyes came open and he stiffened in his chair. Potter had identified the weakest point in their case, one that McPherson was fully aware of. Of course, Baines could have returned that evening, parked at a distance, walked to the house and then murdered Mead, but they currently had no evidence to support that theory.

Kingston didn't respond for several seconds, and when he did, it was with a shrug. 'I think that is enough for now. It is late. Two of my officers will take Ms Baines home.'

'That won't be necessary,' Potter said. 'I shall drive her home myself.'

And with that, she stood up and ushered Baines out of the interview room.

CHAPTER 10

Ngung has gone, and the new woman is much better. I am calling her Lily because I am fed up with these foreign names. She is middle-aged and tough as old boots, with a face like a boot too. No chance of me getting distracted by her charms. I have learned my lesson.

And she is desperate to earn the money, which I will send back to her family in the Philippines. As long as I do that, I will have her absolute loyalty. I have told her to make sure that Kat takes her medication every day. I have warned her that she can be tricky, that I once caught her flushing her pills down the toilet. She is on liquid medication now, which is easier to control, and she seems to prefer it.

So everything is in place. Kat will go into steady decline, and no one will be surprised when she shuffles off her mortal coil. I can get help with that if I need to. I have leverage as they say. In the meantime, all I need to do is tidy up the loose ends and leave the British justice system to deal with Doug Mullen and Becca Baines.

* * *

Wozniak had barely taken off her coat and sat down at her desk before Jim Royce was up on his feet and towering over her, a smirk etched from one side of his face to the other. He leaned low over her desk, so she had to steel herself not to recoil.

'I reckon you're in trouble, my girl,' he hissed. 'The chief super wants you up in his office pronto. And Andy is after your blood as well. You are going to be getting the third degree and no mistake. It'll serve you damn well right.'

She glared back at him. In silence, she got up and, giving him a wide berth, strode out of the office and up the stairs. She had a sense of what it might be about and saw no point in delaying matters. It was unlikely to be a pat-on-the-back meeting, but she felt ready to argue her corner.

When she got to McPherson's lair, she found Kingston as well as the chief superintendent waiting for her. The expressions on their faces were anything but friendly.

'What the hell have you been playing at, Constable?' No politeness, no first names, no names even. McPherson was in a foul mood.

'What do you mean, sir?'

'What I mean is that I asked one of your colleagues to get in touch with Julie Baxter's mother. It became apparent from the conversation they had over the phone that Becca Baines lied when she said it was Julie's mother who gave her the name of Catherine Mead.'

'I see,' Wozniak said, though she didn't see at all. She hadn't known what Becca had or hadn't said. She had been kept well away from the interview and none of the team had told her anything. She felt as though this was deliberate, that she was being isolated.

'So, if she didn't, who did?'

'Why are you asking me?' she said, doing her best to look puzzled.

'Don't play the innocent with us,' Kingston snapped.

'I've just been using my initiative.'

'You mean leaking information to totally inappropriate persons?'

'Andy,' she said, staring right at him. She had no intention of going down without a fight. 'May I remind you that it was you who asked me to go through Julie's diary to see if there were any links between her and Mullen.'

'And were there?'

'Not as far as I can see.'

'Constable!' McPherson's face was a mask of fury. 'This Baines woman has been visiting people named in Julie Baxter's diary. I fail to see how she could have got that information unless you showed her the diary. If you have been sharing that information with Baines, it is highly unprofessional, and very likely a disciplinary matter.'

'May I point out, sir, that it was Becca Baines who went to the Turf Tavern to check out Mullen's story. You see, she wasn't sure whether to believe him or not. Of course, she wanted to believe him, because they are friends, but she had to be sure. And it was while she was doing this that she identified a key witness, namely the man called Alex, who said he had seen Mullen meeting a woman in a green coat. It was this Alex who said he had seen the woman, and that she had eaten two bananas. Becca told me this, so I checked it out myself, and not just what he said about the bananas. The man's description of the woman in the Turf agreed with Mullen's insistence that she was an older woman in her sixties. I was then able to pass all this evidence on to Andy and the team.'

She paused, and took in a deep breath, conscious of the tightrope she was walking. But she plunged on nevertheless. 'So I suppose I thought that I could trust her and that if she wanted to go around asking questions about Julie Baxter's clients in case there was a connection with Mullen or indeed anyone else, then who was I to stop her?'

'You're a police officer. That gave you the right and the duty to conduct these investigations. As a member of the public, she had no such right.'

'Perhaps I made a mistake. I am, of course, not experienced like you or Andy. But I felt strongly that I could trust Ms Baines. Just as Detective Inspector Holden felt she could trust her.'

'Holden?' The name was a red rag to McPherson's bull. 'She is off the case. She is ill. You shouldn't be asking her anything.'

'Sir, she talked to me about Baines before she was removed from the case.'

'Have you been consulting with Holden rather than Andy? Yes or no?'

'I tried to visit Susan, as a colleague and friend, but I was told it was too soon to see her. It is my intention to contact the hospital regularly until I can visit her — unless of course you order me not to.' She sat absolutely still, except for her eyes, which moved from McPherson to Kingston and back to McPherson again. It was, she felt, a smart tactic. He could hardly stop her visiting Holden without showing himself up in a very bad light.

'Go!' he said with an angry wave of the hand. 'If there are no repercussions from this — and I stress the word "if" — you will have to consider yourself extremely fortunate.'

She stood up, nodded at each man and left without a word, shutting the door carefully behind her. In the circumstances, it had gone rather well. And neither of them had asked if she had spoken to Susan Holden by phone. So that was one lie she hadn't had to tell.

* * *

After the dressing down, Wozniak went to the toilets. Her intention was to give herself a good talking-to well away from any men. But she had hardly finished splashing water on her face and applying some cheap perfume a would-be boyfriend had given her when Maddie from Human Resources walked in. She was tall and overweight and had notably short hair. She listened and then offloaded her pearls of wisdom. 'Load of tossers, if you ask me. Half of them have only just come out of the ark, they're frightened of any half-competent woman. Don't you give them an inch. Don't give them anything except a good kick in the balls.' That was exactly the pep talk Wozniak needed and she headed back to her desk reinvigorated, ready to take on anyone and everyone.

All she had to take on at that moment was the pile of paperwork — real and virtual — that cluttered her desk and her inbox. It wasn't until much later, just as she was reaching the point of wanting to go out into the car park and have a good scream, that she received the phone call. The speaker was a woman from the hospital.

'Am I speaking to Krystyna Wozniak?'

'You are.'

'I understand you are Susan Holden's preferred point of contact.'

'Yes,' she replied, although this was the first she had heard of it.

'She was very keen that I should speak to you.'

'How is she?'

'I am pleased to say that she is making progress, though of course there is no knowing how long it'll be before she will be ready for release. But she is now able to receive visitors.'

'You mean, like now?'

'Certainly, if it is convenient.'

'Thank you. Thank you very much.'

She glanced around. The desks nearest to her were deserted, so there was no one to overhear what had been said. Kingston, Royce and several others were attending some training session, from which she had been excluded. 'Someone has to hold the fort,' she had been told by Kingston. Royce, of course, had smirked.

So she rang Maddie, to tell her about Holden. It was as if Maddie were her new best friend. 'Give her my love,' Maddie said. 'And don't worry. If anyone says anything, I'll tell 'em what's what.'

* * *

'Hello, ma'am.'

Susan Holden looked up and for a second or three seemed confused by her visitor.

'Krystyna, ma'am.'

She smiled. 'I do know that. I'm not gaga, just fed up with being here.' She emitted a smile. 'And in case you have forgotten, my name is Susan, and since this is not the police station, you can call me that.'

Wozniak nodded. 'Susan. How are you?'

'I want to go for a walk outside.'

'Is that allowed?'

'You are a policewoman. You are hardly going to let me do a runner.' There was a glint in her eyes that Wozniak found rather unsettling. Holden pointed towards a woman at the door, who was surveying the room as if it were her personal domain. 'That's Sheila, otherwise known as the Dragon. Go and use your charm on her. She likes women in uniform.'

'I am not . . .' Wozniak stopped. This was no time to be splitting hairs.

'She's been watching you ever since you arrived. I expect she's actually more interested in wondering what you would look like without any clothes on.'

Wozniak stood up and walked purposefully towards Sheila, conscious that the woman was watching her every step.

'I'm Susan's colleague from the Thames Valley Police. I wondered if I might take her for a walk in the garden.'

'I'm not sure that's such a good idea.'

'She would like to breathe some fresh air. She wants to stretch her legs, as you English say. And outside we can talk without anyone listening. I think she's feeling a bit paranoid.'

'You're a medical professional too, are you?'

'No, I'm just a human being sensitive to other people's moods and feelings.'

'A bit of a smart-arse then.'

'You're not the first to say that.'

This seemed to amuse her, because she smiled. Wozniak waited.

'You and her want some privacy, do you now?'

'Yes.'

'You lovers then?'

For a split second Wozniak was thrown off balance. 'Would it make any difference if we were?'

'I'm just curious.'

'So can I take her out into the garden or not?'

Sheila moved closer to Wozniak, so close that she got a strong whiff of the woman's body odour. 'Listen. I don't trust your Susan. Not one tiny bit. So let me make this very clear. From the time she steps out of this ward to the time she returns, she remains your responsibility. One little thing goes wrong, and I'll pin you to the wall. You get my drift?'

'I get your drift, Sheila. But don't you worry, I can handle her.'

Sheila gave a wry smile. 'I think it may be the other way round, sweetie.'

Half an hour later, after several fast-paced circuits of the extensive grounds, they sat down on a bench under a spreading oak tree. Wozniak was panting somewhat and, despite the cool air, sweating from the exertion. By contrast, Holden's breathing was steady and untroubled, unlike her hands, which buzzed with energy and seemed unable to settle. 'Krystyna,' she said, 'I want you to give me a full update.'

'Of course.' She had been half expecting this, and so she had all the key facts lined up inside her head, or rather all the facts that she had been able to glean, both by listening in to conversations between her colleagues and also asking questions while visiting the ladies' toilets. On one occasion she had even exchanged flippant remarks with Royce over the water cooler in the hope of encouraging an indiscretion. But he had been as closed as a clam. She wondered if there might not be some unwelcome repercussions from that in the future.

Holden listened intently to the torrent of information, occasionally butting in with a question, but otherwise silent except for the occasional "I see."

When Wozniak came to halt, Holden nodded enthusiastically. 'Very good, Krystyna.'

'Thank you, Susan.'

'So McPherson and Kingston think Becca and Doug are in it together?'

'Everyone else seems to think that as well.'

'Including you, Krystyna?'

'I am keeping an open mind.'

'Good.'

'There is one other thing. I have been maybe a bit stupid, but I met Becca and I gave her Julie Baxter's diary.'

'Why?'

'Because I am not able to pursue the contacts in it myself. DI Kingston says it is a low priority, and he gives me lots of other boring work. He is trying to sideline me from the investigation because I ask too many questions. Poor Becca is desperate to help Doug.'

'That was very foolish. If they find out, you will be in serious trouble.'

'Yes.'

'You are very brave to take the risk.'

'Am I? Not just stupid?'

'Definitely not just stupid!'

'Really?'

'But now, I hope, you can be stupid and brave again.' Holden said nothing but began to scrabble about in her pocket. She pulled out her hand and opened her fingers. There were four pills on her palm.

'They treat you like a zombie in here. Sleep, sleep and more sleep. But they are easy to fool. It is child's play to take one pill, but not the second one.'

'Is that wise? I am sure they know what they are doing.'

Holden made a guttural noise and spat onto the grass. Then she gripped Wozniak by the wrist, her fingernails digging in so hard that Wozniak yelped with pain.

'I have to escape from here,' Holden hissed.

'You make it sound like a prison.'

'As good as. So the question is — will you help me or will you stop me?'

Wozniak opened her mouth but realized that she wasn't at all sure what to say. Was it responsible to let Susan abscond when she had stopped taking her prescribed dosage of medication? How stable was she? She knew so little about her, except what people had told her, which meant that it was hard for her to know what would classify as "normal" behaviour in Holden's case.

'I know what you're thinking, Krystyna. That I'm being irresponsible. You probably think I am a bit mad. But look!' She opened her hand again to reveal the four pills. 'If you don't trust me, you take them and you administer them to me. I promise that I will take one in the morning and one in the evening over the next forty-eight hours. After that you can bring me back here and I won't play up. I promise.'

Wozniak still didn't answer. She knew what she ought to do, what her duty was, and yet . . .

Holden wasn't going to give up. 'Please, Krystyna, I need to do this for Becca and Doug. I will not abandon them in their hour of need.' She paused and, when she still didn't get a reply, she applied another layer of emotional blackmail. 'If you refuse to help, if they are imprisoned for something they didn't do, how will you be able to live with yourself, Krystyna?'

Wozniak thought about that, tried to imagine Mullen and Baines as a pair of devious killers, and failed. The fact was she quite liked both of them. 'All right,' she said. 'You win.'

'Bless you.' Without warning, she took Wozniak's hand and like an Elizabethan courtier greeting his queen, kissed the back of it, an act that threw Wozniak completely off balance.

* * *

Becca Baines was sitting on a kitchen chair in her tiny garden at the back of the house drinking a cup of tea when a fast-approaching car squealed to a halt at the front of the house.

'Not again!' she expostulated to Rex, who pricked up his ears, but showed no sign of behaving like a proper guard dog, neither growling or barking. Indeed, as a car door clicked open, he ran round the corner wagging his tail in greeting. Becca got to her feet, preparing to rain a volley of abuse upon whichever police officers had come to bother her again, and was amazed to find the dog lying on his back, with Holden vigorously rubbing his stomach. The car was already retreating down the lane.

'You!' she said.

'Me,' Holden said.

'I thought you were . . . were in the hospital.'

'I've escaped.'

'You what?'

'With a bit of help.'

'From whom?'

Holden ignored the question, instead holding out her hand. On its palm lay four pills. 'I promised I would hand these over to you. You have to make sure I take one pill twice a day, so that I don't go doolally.'

'Who did you promise this to?'

'It doesn't matter. If I don't tell you, then you can't dump him or her in the shit.' She grinned. Her eyes looked as though they had gone for a walk on the wild side and weren't coming back any time soon. 'Becca, is it OK if I stay here for a couple of nights? You see, the first place they are going to look for me is in my own home, so I cannot stay there.'

'What if they come looking for you here?'

'I think that is unlikely.'

'Or they come looking for me again. I have already been questioned once.'

A rather manic smile creased Holden's face. 'Well if they do, I am sure I can rely on you to put them off the scent. I can, can't I?'

'You mean lie? I'm a nurse. I can't just—'

'You can use your own judgement.' She stepped forward, took Becca's hand. She placed the four pills on her palm, then gently folded her fingers over it. 'There. You are in charge of my medication, and I promise I will be as good as gold.'

Becca opened her fingers to inspect the pills. She reckoned she knew what they might be, but she wasn't going to ask. What was obvious was that Holden should have been taking them and had managed to fool the hospital staff. How many should she be taking? Four pills would cover two days at the most. Probably she needed two pills twice a day. Reluctantly, Becca took them and slipped them in her pocket. She needed to find somewhere safe to keep them.

'Thank you, my dear,' Holden said. Her face and her voice were those of a little girl pretending she hadn't been naughty. 'Anyway, I wonder if there's any chance of a meal before too much longer? I haven't eaten a thing since breakfast.'

* * *

'Becca, how nice to hear from you again.' Leo's voice was as smooth and ingratiating as ever.

She had gone outside on the pretext of walking Rex. 'Just a quick one,' she had promised Holden. 'I'll be back in ten minutes.' What trouble could the woman get up to in ten minutes? Probably quite a lot. She didn't want her suddenly running off into the night. But Holden, with the food inside her, plus a pill, which she had taken under Becca's strict supervision, had slumped down on the sofa bed and was soon watching an episode of *Endeavour*, giggling happily.

So Becca had gone off with Rex, satisfied that she had taken all sensible precautions. Only when she had put a good distance between herself and the house did she ring Leo.

'Seeing you again,' Leo began, 'reminded me of how much fun you could be.'

'Cut the flannel, Leo.'

'Ah, I take it this call isn't because you are missing me then.'

'I need you to swear, Leo, on your mother's grave, that everything I say to you will remain totally confidential.'

'That hardly seems necessary. Is there something wrong with you? I am already bound by my Hippocratic oath to respect a patient's confidentiality.'

'Just promise me. Say it out loud.'

'I promise you, Becca. Now, what is wrong with you?'

'It's not me,' she said, and explained the situation. She had barely started before he butted in.

'You need to take DI Holden back to the hospital. For her own good.'

'I promised her she could stay here. And you promised to help me. You know who to talk to. You can find out what drug regimen she is on, and you can get me some more medication. Then I will look after her here for a few days until she is stabilized.'

'It's highly irregular.'

'Maybe, but it's the best way of keeping her safe. She trusts me, and as long as I can keep her here with me, then I have a good chance of helping her recover. But I will need some more meds for her by the end of tomorrow.'

'You make it sound easy.'

'Easy or hard, will you do it? Yes or no?'

The line went quiet. 'Yes.'

'And you will keep it secret, yes?'

'In so far as I can.'

'Nobody must know she is staying with me.'

'No, I understand that.'

'Good. Thanks, Leo. Just ring me when you've got it sorted and I'll meet you wherever you like.'

'Got to go,' he said, and terminated the call.

CHAPTER 11

We had dinner together the other night. Or was it last night? I get confused. Usually, I eat in the kitchen, with Ngung, or rather it is Lily now. I prefer the kitchen. It is warm and cosy in there. But he prefers to eat in the dining room, sometimes with me and sometimes with visitors. The table is long, and we sit there like Lord and Lady Muck, him at one end and me at the other. It feels rather grand. It reminds me of my parents. They always ate their evening meal in the dining room. When I was older, I was occasionally allowed to stay up and eat with them there. That was a real treat.

'Have you been behaving yourself?' he said.

'I think so.'

'Lily says you have.'

'Does she? Then I must have been.'

He picked up his mobile phone. He was always looking at his phone. I am not sure why. No one had rung him. I don't like mobile phones. They are so complicated.

'Is Ngung having a nice holiday?' I asked. My mother instilled in me the importance of making polite conversation at dinner. 'It is rude to sit in silence, my girl,' she used to say.

He stopped fiddling with his phone and looked at me. He seemed puzzled.

'Is Ngung having a nice holiday,' I repeated loudly in case he hadn't heard me clearly the first time.

'I expect she is. Hasn't she sent you a postcard? You had better ask Lily.'

The clock on the sideboard began to chime. I counted the chimes right up to seven, though the hands of the clock said it was eight. Never mind. It used to belong to my mother, but now it is mine. It is a very special one. My mother told me it was very expensive, but I don't care about that. I like it because it is lovely, and had been her mother's before it was hers.

I wanted to ask him if there was something wrong with it, but he was looking at his wretched phone again. I felt really rather cross. It wasn't polite at all. My mother never let Father do that. I had one prawn left on my plate. I like to leave the best until last. So I put that in my mouth and savoured it. It was delicious. I put my knife and fork down and looked directly at him. 'Where's my coat?' I said.

That made him look up. 'Your coat? Which coat?'

'The green coat. I am fed up with the blue one.'

'The green coat is perfectly safe. I've had it cleaned.'

'Can I see it?'

'Another night. I have work to do.'

He looked down at his phone again. I would like to have taken it from him and thrown it down the toilet. I did that once and he got very cross. Very cross indeed.

'Why can't I see it now?'

He glared at me. He was getting cross now. I could see it in his eyes. He picked up the little bell, which always sat next to him on the table, and rang it. 'I think it must be time for Lily to give you your medicine,' he said.

* * *

There was an obvious person for Leo Francombe to contact. He hesitated at first, not at all sure how James Elworthy would react to his request. But as it happened, he turned out to be very helpful.

'Sorry to ring so early, James,' he said, 'but I have a small favour to ask. Off the record.'

'OK, tell me what it is, but no promises.'

So Francombe explained.

He waited. There was an ominously long silence before Elworthy replied. 'I will see what I can do,' he said briskly, 'but as you are aware this is highly irregular, so nothing should be committed to text or voice message in case it comes back to bite me. Are you with me, Leo?'

'Of course.'

'I can justify it to myself in terms of being in the patient's best interests, but not everyone would see it that way.'

'Absolutely. That is how I see it, and the last thing I want to do is cause myself problems too. Any idea of when and where?'

'Let's say ten a.m. in the car park.'

'Fine.'

'Just don't be late. I have a busy day in front of me.'

Francombe felt it had gone well. Elworthy had been cooperative and yet very careful. Careful was very much in his character, cooperative less so, but they had known each other since university. They had been friends then, though also rivals, both playing rugby for the Greyhounds, and both hoping to make it into the blues for the match against Cambridge. That shared history and medical training tied them together.

* * *

Becca was feeling guilty. Not because she had lied to Holden about why she was going out. Not because she had left Rex in the detective inspector's dubious care. But because she had double-dosed her. Leo had texted her to say he'd have the medication mid-morning and offered to deliver it then, so she didn't need to string the remaining pills out. So in that case it seemed only sensible to get Holden back on her prescribed dose.

It was easy as pie getting the second pill into her. Holden had happily eaten a small bowl of porridge prepared for her by Becca's loving hands, with added Greek yoghurt, forest fruits and a second crushed pill inside it. And by the time Becca was ready to leave on her mission, Holden was back in bed, sleeping a silent, untroubled sleep. Becca took her wrist and checked the pulse, before padding silently downstairs. She gave Rex a final chance to pee, then locked him in and got into her car.

Before she set off, she put her phone on silent. The last thing she wanted was to be bothered by Holden, or indeed by Leo. She would ring him later when she had completed her mission and returned to check on Holden. As long as she got the medication from Leo by the evening, that was all that mattered.

She had a plan in place and a list of four addresses all in or near Oxford. Checking each one out shouldn't take long. When Holden finally got up, she could ring her if she became agitated. Becca had printed her number on a note, along with information about watering and walking Rex, and what food was available. She might be angry when she realized that she had been left alone with the dog, but hopefully with the increased medication she wouldn't want to do anything much except collapse in front of the TV again.

The first address was in Wytham village, just to the west of the A34 as it heads north past Oxford. This turned out to be a beautiful stone house occupied by a Katerine with a strong Mancunian accent and a very distinct limp. Both seemed to rule her out as Mullen's mysterious Kat in a green coat, and Katerine told her she had decided to let her niece cut her hair when it really needed doing. 'I don't need anything fancy like. And it all adds up when you 'ave it done too often.' After downing a cup of strong tea and a couple of ginger biscuits, Becca made her excuses and left.

Catherine number two was more promising, softly spoken, mid- to late fifties, and smartly dressed. On this particular day, however, she had been a blue-and-yellow person, not a green one. 'I write romantic novels,' she confided as Becca embarked on another cup of tea — Earl Grey this time. 'I try to avoid going into Oxford if I can, and when I saw Julie's advertisement in the local free newspaper, I realized that if she came to my house to cut my hair, it would save me a lot of time and allow me to focus on my writing.' She dropped her voice dramatically, as if her publisher might have bugged her room and was monitoring the number of keystrokes per day. 'My publisher gets agitated if I don't deliver two novels a year. I must say, this writing lark really is a bit of a treadmill sometimes.'

* * *

Susan Holden was dreaming. It was one of those dreams where you know you are dreaming, and you desperately want it to end. She screamed. Not that anyone would hear, because — of course — she was screaming inside her dream. She knew she had to wake up. There was something she had to do, and she couldn't do that while she was dreaming.

She yelled again, but again it had no effect. She was stuck inside the dream. Suppose she could never get out? What then? She had to rescue someone, someone in prison. But who the hell was it?

She was in a house, no, not a house, a building, like . . . like the huge block of classrooms at her school. Was it her school? The problem was she couldn't find the stairs with the metal banisters that led down to the ground floor and the exit doors.

She wanted to cry, but she had never been a crybaby and she wasn't going to start now. And then she heard something, a soft persistent noise that got louder and louder until suddenly she was awake. The sound had stopped. She found herself in an unfamiliar bed and hanging above her was a lampshade made of red cardboard or something, which she definitely didn't recognize. The noise started again, and after the second buzz, she realized it was her phone. She forced herself upright, saw the handset on the side table and picked it up.

'Yes?'

'How are you?' The voice was female, but she couldn't put a name to it.

'Who is this?'

'Krystyna.'

The name rang a bell and yet . . . She couldn't get her mind to work. The stupid thing wouldn't tell her who this Christina was.

'Do I know you?'

There was a pause. Quite a long pause, she thought. 'Detective Constable Krystyna Wozniak.'

'Yes. Yes, of course.'

'Are you all right, ma'am? Are you taking your pills like you promised?'

'My pills. Yes, I . . . I . . .' And then she realized why she was feeling like she was, like she had when they first put her on medication, before she had started to only take one, not two.

'Ma'am . . . Susan . . . are you OK?'

Holden exploded. 'The bitch. That bitch Becca has drugged me.'

'But you promised to take your medication. One pill twice a day.'

Holden's brain had gone into fast-forward mode. 'But not two twice a day. She must have put a second pill in my porridge. No wonder I feel so half-baked.'

'Susan, can I help?' Wozniak was saying, but Holden wasn't listening. She was feeling in the pockets of her trousers on the chair, she was hurrying down the stairs and then scouring the room, she was scrabbling in her coat, which was hanging on a peg by the door. She opened the door, ignoring the blast of cold air which met her. Then she screamed.

'The bitch has taken my car keys!'

'Susan? Ma'am?' Wozniak was uncertain which form of address was best in the circumstances. 'I drove you to Becca's yesterday. Your car must be at your house. Maybe your keys are there too?'

'What? Did you?'

'I did.'

Holden subsided onto one of the chairs at the kitchen table, all her anger suddenly spent. 'Of course.'

'Actually, ma'am, I've got some news. Good news.'

'What?'

'They are releasing Doug Mullen. One of the girls told me.'

'Why?'

'The rumour is that McPherson is getting cold feet about the evidence.'

Holden tried to process this, to understand the whys and wherefores, but her brain was reluctant to cooperate. She needed help.

'What are you doing today, Krystyna?'

'Cars, ma'am. They've put me on following up on burned-out cars. A vital job, apparently.'

'In that case, Constable, I suggest you come and check out a car that has been set on fire just down the lane here.'

'Really?'

'Not really, but I am reporting it now. I am not going to tell you who I am and you are not going to waste valuable time tracing the source of the call. Like a good detective you are going to use your initiative and drive over here to investigate.'

'I understand, ma'am.'

'Thank heavens for small mercies.'

* * *

It had all happened so suddenly. One moment Mullen was lying half asleep on his bunk, dreaming of Rex, but when he picked the dog up, he had — alarmingly — morphed into a white cat.

The next moment there was an insistent banging on the cell door and one of the guards was telling him he had five minutes to get dressed and gather up his things. Then he was escorted through the prison, given back the possessions they had removed from him on his arrival, and before he knew it he was outside in the road, looking up at a grey sky, and feeling mightily relieved.

He turned left and walked up the slope towards what he knew to be the main road. There would, he assumed, be a bus stop somewhere, and from there he could make his way home. Home. The word was full of possibilities. Would Becca be there? Had she been told he was being released? Given that she wasn't here to pick him up, he guessed maybe not. He pictured her reaction when he appeared unannounced, the intensity of her hug, probably tears even. Of course, if his mobile hadn't run completely flat, he could have rung her, but things are what they are, he told himself, reciting the words he had learned at the knee of his long-dead great-aunt Maud.

The memory of his aunt was comforting, the present more sobering. The sky above had darkened and, party pooper that it was, rain had started to fall. Only then did he realize that he hadn't entered prison with a waterproof coat and so he hadn't come out with one either. He didn't care. He would soon be on a bus and what harm could a bit of rain do anyway?

The answer to that unspoken question was that rain that falls in torrents can pretty quickly drench you right through to your underwear. By the time he reached the bus stop (no protective roof and no timetable indicating when a bus might arrive), he was beginning to feel a bit sorry for himself. But he was not a man to give up at the first sign of trouble. A bus would surely come soon.

As it was, what did come soon was not a bus but a good Samaritan in a blue Skoda, an eager grin across his face. 'Need a lift?'

'Where are you going?' Mullen replied.

'Oxford,' he said. 'I passed the bus you're waiting for. Broken down on the hill at Bix.'

Mullen got in, muttering his thanks.

'You've not just climbed over the wire, have you? Or tunnelled your way out.' The guy was clearly a comedian with a bad sense of timing and a limited sense of humour. But Mullen didn't care. It wasn't raining inside the car.

'I was on remand, but they've just released me,' he admitted.

'Welcome back to the world. I was in there once. I won't tell you what for — or I might have to kill you!' He laughed, as if he had just invented the funniest joke ever.

'It's kind of you to stop.'

'I know what it's like,' he said, suddenly serious. 'So, where do you want to be? Oxford itself or . . . ?'

'Could you maybe drop me near Wallingford?'

'No problemo,' the joker said.

Mullen tried playing silent and tired and, to his relief, it appeared to work. The guy stopped chattering and joking, and Mullen nodded off. More than nodded off, in fact, because he was suddenly woken by his rescuer volleying a series of swear words into his mobile phone.

'Sorry, mate, change of plan. Got to drive to Aylesbury. God only knows why. Tell you what, I'll drop you up here at Stadhampton. Best I can do. I'll be dead meat if I don't get there fast.'

So that was that. Out into the rain again, a quick "hasta la vista" and the guy was off into the distance, water spraying out behind him, while Mullen gave an unconvincing wave of thanks to the fast-disappearing car.

* * *

Holden looked down at her feet. Rex was sitting there, ever so cute, and pleading to go out. She was rather pleased with the fact that she had given the mutt his breakfast and that he had eaten it up. But the last thing she wanted was for him to shit on the kitchen floor or the rug. She went to the door and let him out. The wind had strengthened since she had stood there a few minutes ago screaming blue murder. She shivered, but it was an unconscious act because her attention was elsewhere. She had just realized that she was wearing an unfamiliar nightdress.

It was far too big for her. She preferred something crisp and white, not this deep purple one, which hung around her like a shapeless sack. And yet there was something about it that echoed back to her childhood. She stood on her toes. She began to twirl round, lifting her arms, allowing the material to billow round her, and in that moment she felt free. She squealed with joy, like a schoolgirl dancing in a spring meadow. Rex reappeared from wherever he had gone and, picking up her mood, began to run around her, yapping and jumping like an over-energetic puppy. She kneeled down and scooped him up and ruffled his fur. 'Time for me to have a shower, I think.'

Back inside the cottage, she ferreted in the fridge and found a three-quarters-empty carton of juice. She was so thirsty that she drained it without bothering to pour it into a glass. Some splashed on the nightie, but she didn't care. And then she heard the sound of a car pulling up. Krystyna must have been driving flat out. Or maybe she herself had lost all sense of time? She opened the door, and Rex went racing past her ankles, giving a fine impression of a guard dog.

But it was not Krystyna. It was a man. He got out of the car and offered Rex the back of his hand. Rex sniffed it, and then licked it — not much of a guard dog after all. The man was tall and thickset. Holden tensed, suddenly on guard. She felt vulnerable, out here on her own, dressed in a tent-like nightie.

'Is Becca here?' the man said, his eyes taking her in.

She shook her head. She stood in the doorway, her mind frantically scrambling around the room behind her, trying to recall anything that might serve as a weapon, though her eyes remained fixed firmly on the man. Where were the kitchen knives? She couldn't remember seeing them, but there had to be one somewhere — a drawer most likely. Or what about a saucepan? Improvise with whatever there is available. The words of her self-defence trainer kicked in. Improvise or die.

'Who the hell are you?' she snapped. Don't show any vulnerability.

'I think you must be Detective Inspector Susan Holden.' *How on earth does he know me?*

'You haven't answered my question.' *Don't give your assailant an inch.*

'I thought I would find you here.' Who told him? Becca? Krystyna? Surely not.

'I have something for you.' The man held out his hand. There was a small white box in it. 'I have not come here to drag you back to hospital. Becca asked me to get some medication for you so you wouldn't have to go back there.' So it was Becca! At least it wasn't Krystyna.

'I am taking a risk in doing this, but Becca was insistent.' Holden was barely listening. Why? Why had Becca betrayed her?

The man continued to speak with exaggerated calmness. 'Becca said she would look after you herself. She said it was important. So I—'

'Put the pills on the table,' she hissed, and waited until he had done so. 'You still haven't told me who the hell you are!'

He smiled. Under the circumstances it could have been the smile of a tiger. 'I am Leo,' he said. 'Leo Francombe. One of Becca's friends.'

'I don't believe you.'

'I am a consultant at the Oxford University Hospitals NHS Trust. As you no doubt know, she is an Accident and Emergency nurse. Rather a good one, as it happens. She has been off work since she lost her baby at birth.' He paused, and a look of sadness passed across his face. 'I believe I was the baby's father. But I failed her when she needed me. So this time, when she asked me to help, I wasn't going to fail her again.'

Francombe looked up. Dark clouds had massed above them, and suddenly rain began to fall. Not a light shower, but a torrent that threatened to drench them both. Holden was still eyeing him warily, but she suddenly shrugged and retreated inside the house. She left the door open and after a moment's hesitation, Francombe followed her inside.

Holden stood backed up against the kitchen sink, facing him. She had managed to purloin a short, red-handled knife from the sink and was now holding it up. He seemed nervous, a good thing as far as she was concerned.

'Thank you for the pills. There really is no need for you to hang around here now.'

'Where is Becca?'

'Not in, as you can see.'

'She's not answering her phone.'

'Perhaps she's busy and has put it on silent.'

'She was meant to meet me, so I could hand over the medication I just gave you. I've rung her. I've texted her. Nothing.'

'Why don't you try again?'

'OK.' He rang, but again there was no response. He swore.

'Maybe it's broken. Or has a flat battery.'

'Unlikely, I would say.'

'Why is it unlikely?' *Keep him talking. Watch his every move. Be ready to do whatever is necessary for your survival.*

'Because she rang me last night and insisted I ring her back this morning, once I had sourced some medication for you. So I did.'

'And?'

'It's unlike her not to answer, especially when she'd asked me to call.'

Francombe sounded genuinely worried, but Holden wasn't about to be fooled. 'What is unlike her? To switch off her phone? Or to allow it to go flat? Or to break it?'

'To not meet me today as planned. Look, when she rang last night, she was desperate to source some medication for you. She promised to meet me wherever I said. But she never did and now she is out of contact.'

153

'Point taken. But right now, you have handed over the medication directly to me, so all's well that ends well. As for me, I need to have a shower, and I am not going to do that until you have gone.' She held the knife up. 'And don't imagine for a moment that I won't use this. So I will say this just once: it is time you got into your flash Harry car and made yourself scarce.'

He looked at her. 'Are you sure you don't know where she is?'

'I'm sure.'

He shrugged and made his way to the door. She followed him, and stood in the doorway until he had disappeared from view. She stood there for five minutes, to ensure he didn't return. Only then did she lock and bolt the door and make her way upstairs to have her shower. The demons were still buzzing in her head and they were all telling her one thing: "Don't trust the smart-arse."

* * *

Becca wondered if the next address might be a case of third time lucky. It was a bit of a long shot, but there weren't so many potential Kats that she could afford not to give them all a try. Or was what she was doing a waste of time? Sitting in the car before leaving for her next destination, she checked her mobile. No calls from Holden. Maybe she was still asleep. But there were two missed called from Leo, but what the hell. She would get the medication off him later. Right now, there were more important things to do.

This time her destination turned out to be an altogether more imposing house. It was situated in Boars Hill and was surrounded by a tall stone wall. Nothing too unusual in this highly sought-after area. Electric gates (shut, of course) discouraged casual callers and two bells differentiated between "Tradesmen" and "Friends," as if there were no other possibilities. Irritation flickered through Becca. Would paramedics on their way to save a life be classified as tradesmen then?

Or a community nurse? She clenched her teeth and pressed the "Friends" bell.

The gates opened and she drove in. She stopped and got out of the car wondering if someone would come out to check who she was but no one did. There were security cameras visible, so it seemed more likely that someone was watching her via a laptop screen and the comfort of a high-end office chair. She gathered herself together and made her way to the front door. Rather than a button to press, there was a long metal bellpull to the right, so she grabbed it and pulled it down hard. She heard a low-tech jangle of sound from indoors and waited. Silence. Was no one in? There were two garages with dark green doors, so the absence of any car on the drive did not necessarily mean they weren't there.

She was about to ring again when, to her surprise, the door opened. The woman looking out at her was short and stout. Middle-aged and business-like, stern even.

'Who are you?' English was clearly not her first language.

'I understand a lady lives here who has her hair cut by Julie Baxter. Is that you?'

'No.'

'I think the lady's name is Catherine?'

'Julie not come anymore. Gone away.'

'Perhaps I could speak to Catherine. I am a friend of Julie's. Perhaps I could be Catherine's hairdresser.'

'I can cut hair. No need to pay extra.'

'But can I just speak to Catherine?'

'Mrs not well. You go now.'

Becca paused. The woman clearly didn't want to let her in. She might or might not have a genuine reason for this, but her reluctance only made Becca more determined to get in. The question was: how?

'I need to go to the toilet.'

The woman's face hardened even further. 'Mr not like it if you come in. You must go.'

'I had baby,' Becca said suddenly, slipping into the same simplified English as the woman. 'She die at birth.

My bladder go bad.' She pointed expressively at her crotch. 'Please. I need to go to toilet. Or I wet my pants.'

Her eyes welled up with tears, which was no piece of acting. Just to speak of Alice, even in such a duplicitous manner, brought all the agony flooding back.

'Sorry,' the woman said. She moved back a step into the house as if she was about to shut the door. 'Very sorry for your baby. Very sad.' She beckoned to her. 'You come in quickly for toilet.'

The toilet was inside the front door to the right, and the woman took up position nearby as if she had been taught to regard all uninvited guests as criminals. But when Becca re-emerged a few minutes later — and she really was glad to have had a pee — the woman had disappeared from her post. There was the sound of voices deeper inside the house, so Becca made her way towards it.

The woman was standing next to the kitchen table talking to another woman, who was seated. 'Where is she?' the woman was saying.

'I am here,' Becca broke in. 'Your . . . your maid kindly allowed me to use your toilet.'

'You?' The woman frowned. 'You are not Julie.' She turned back to the woman. 'Lily, where is Julie? I demand to know.'

'She has gone.'

'Where has she gone? Why does no one ever tell me anything?'

'She not coming here anymore.' Lily was clearly alarmed by what was happening. She turned to Becca. 'Please, madam, you must leave. Now.'

'Kat?' Becca said.

The woman turned back to her again, responding to the name. She stared at Becca, as if trying to work out who this intruder was. 'Do I know you?'

'No. But my friend Doug knows you. He met you once in a pub in Oxford. The Turf Tavern. Do you remember?'

'Doug? I don't think I know anyone called Doug.'

156

'He had a little black dog with him.'

The frown on Kat's face slowly transformed into a smile of recollection. 'Oh yes! I do. He was a lovely dog. He sat on my lap while Doug bought me a drink.' She laughed. 'I guess you would call him a lap dog.'

'Mrs, it is time for you to take your medicine,' Lily said sharply, trying to get the situation under control. 'And you, Madam, you must leave before you get Mrs and me into trouble.'

Trouble? The word sent a shiver of apprehension through Becca. Trouble from whom? And why? But just to ask herself the question was to receive an answer. Because this was the Kat that Doug had met in the pub. Because the Julie who came to cut Kat's hair had been brutally murdered. And what about the other dead woman, the woman she had found in the old barn? Who was she? The answer was lurking in the depths of her subconscious, fighting its way to the surface, but so was fear. She needed to leave. This was more than she could handle. She was a nurse, not a detective. It was stupid of her to imagine she could solve the mystery of the woman in the green coat — and yet she had. She had found her. But she was afraid because it was patently obvious that the maid was frightened too.

'Yes, of course, I'll go,' she said hastily. 'I am very sorry to have bothered you both. I will go and I won't come back.'

She picked up her bag and swung it over her shoulder. 'Thank you.'

Kat and Lily were looking at her with fascination. No, not fascination, something else. But what? Becca stopped. 'Is everything all right?'

Of course it isn't! The thought flashed through her brain like an electric current. And the two women were not look-ing at her either. They were looking at someone behind her. She tried to turn, to see who it was, but that person's arm was suddenly round her throat, and she was being pulled backwards, and she couldn't shake herself free. There was something else, a pungent smell that she knew all too well from her work as a nurse. A hand pressed something damp over her face. It stank of chloroform, and though she knew she had to resist, she couldn't. She wanted to scream, to cry out, but it was too late. She disappeared into oblivion.

* * *

Holden had just stepped out of the shower when she heard an insistent banging on the downstairs door and an answering yap, yap, yap from the dog. 'Hang on!' she yelled. It had to be Wozniak. She could surely wait for a couple of minutes.

She dried herself methodically. She found some talcum powder in the bathroom cupboard and dusted herself all over. She stood in front of the cupboard mirror and examined her face, alarmed at what she saw. The wide-open eyes made her look just a little bit . . . well, mad. More than a little, if she was honest.

Downstairs, Wozniak was hammering on the door again. Holden swore, wrapped herself in the large towel Becca had left at the bottom of her bed and made her way downstairs. She hesitated. Suppose it wasn't Wozniak? Suppose it was someone else — Leo Francombe again for example? She didn't trust him. He was too smooth to be taken at face value. She picked up the red-handled knife again — just in case. Or maybe it was someone from the hospital, come to take her back. Seeing her walking around with a knife in her hand would only make it worse. She would certainly not use it on them — she wasn't that sort of person. And yet . . .

The internal wrangling continued, and when she did open the door, the knife was still in her hand.

It wasn't Wozniak. A bedraggled figure entered, water pouring off him.

'Doug!' She gave an alarming squeal, which might have meant anything.

'Susan?' Mullen's eyes flickered from her face to the knife and back again. 'Are you going to use that?'

'What?'

'The knife.'

She looked down at her hand as if seeing it for the first time. She laughed. 'Oh, no, sorry! I wasn't sure who you might be. I mean, I thought it might be a doctor or my police colleague or maybe the killer. You really can't be too careful. But you are the last person I was expecting to see!'

'I've been released.'

'Krystyna told me you were going to be.'

'And this is where I live.'

'I suppose it is.'

'So, might I ask what exactly you are doing here?'

'I stayed over last night.'

'Here?'

'I slept in Becca's bed. She looked after me ever so well.' She gave Mullen a wicked little smile, then laughed rather wildly. 'Not what you're thinking, Doug. She's all yours if you want her. You see, when I scarpered from the psychiatric hospital, I needed somewhere to go, so I came here.'

Mullen stretched out a hand. 'Please, Susan, would you give me the knife?'

'Yes, of course.' She handed it over to him, handle first. 'Doug, you do know that I would never hurt you?'

Mullen went over to the kitchen drawer and put the knife away. 'I was more concerned about you hurting yourself. Tell me why you were in hospital in the first place, and why did you do a runner?'

'It's a long story.'

'I'm not in a hurry. How about we talk about it over a mug of tea?' He switched on the kettle.

'Have you spoken to Becca since you were released?'

'My mobile is dead. I'd better charge it up.' He felt in his pockets, went over to where he kept his charger and plugged the phone in.

'She isn't answering her phone,' Holden said. 'She was meant to meet a guy called Leo Francombe today. He was going to access some more medication for me, but when she didn't answer his calls, he brought it here himself.'

'Did she tell you anything else about where she might be going, apart from meeting Leo?' Mullen had given up on making tea. The mention of Leo Francombe had thrown him off kilter.

'She didn't tell me anything.' Holden grinned as if this were the funniest thing in the world. 'We had breakfast together. She gave me one of my pills, but actually I reckon she slipped another one into my porridge because I fell fast asleep in bed and didn't wake until much later.'

'She didn't leave a note?'

'No.'

'And you've no idea where she might have gone?'

'No.'

Whatever had happened to Mullen while he was in custody, he had come out with his capacity to ask questions unimpaired — though maybe not his tea-making ability. Holden went over to the cupboard and scrabbled around until she found a packet of ginger biscuits. A couple of minutes later, they each had a mug of tea and three biscuits neatly stacked in front of them. They sat there sipping and crunching for some time, engulfed in silence, until Holden sat up sharply.

'Wozniak! Where the hell is she?'

'Sorry?'

'My constable. She should have been here long before now!'

'Perhaps she's been delayed.'

'Of course she's been delayed!' Holden was now up on her feet and pacing around like a caged wild animal. 'But I need her. She's my only ally in the force.'

'What do you need her for?' Mullen took a large bite out of his second biscuit. He was trying to exude calmness. Whatever pills Holden was or wasn't on, she was certainly damn excitable. If they were meant to calm her down, they weren't doing a very good job.

'It's not a question of what I need her for. It's why the hell isn't she here.'

'There's probably a good reason.'

'Stop being so blooming calm, Doug! Have you any idea how annoying that is?'

'Sorry,' he said, because what else could he say.

'Krystyna Wozniak, the only officer in the force who has my back, has gone missing. Question one: why? Question two: how come Becca did not meet Leo Francombe as planned earlier today? Question three, why is Becca not answering her phone? Does not all of that seem bloody odd? Alarming even.'

'Let me try ringing Becca now,' Mullen said, getting up from the table. He needed to calm Holden down, and if he got Becca on the phone, that would surely help. But much as he hoped to hear her cheerful "Hi, Doug!" and so provide a simple explanation for at least two of Holden's anxieties, the fact was that the call went straight into her answering service.

'I see what you mean,' Mullen said, his face set in a frown.

'There is one other thing that's odd about today,' Holden said, as her brain engaged with a theory that had been growing with terrifying speed inside her head. In other circumstances she might not have voiced this theory without first giving it very careful consideration, but Holden wasn't in any frame of mind to pander to such niceties. 'Today is the day you were released from custody.'

'What are you talking about?'

'What time were you released, Doug?'

'What time? What has that got to do with anything?'

'I may have flipped my lid.' Holden was up on her feet, rocking backwards and forwards. Mullen was reminded of an elephant he had seen in a wildlife park, so distressed that it rocked in much the same way. 'In many ways I hope that I have. Because the alternative is much, much worse.'

'Susan.' Mullen was up on his feet too. Holden seemed to have departed to another galaxy, and he wasn't sure how to bring her back to earth. 'Try not to alarm yourself.'

These words seemed to strike a chord, because she reached out and grabbed Mullen's hand. 'I'm trying not to

alarm you, Doug. But please answer me this question, however stupid it seems to you. What time were you released
from custody today?'

* * *

Holden had listened in silence to Mullen's account, though
she still displayed clear signs of agitation — a sudden movement, a shaking of her head, a sharp acceleration in her
breathing. He was tempted to ask when her next dose of pills
was due but realized this was unlikely to be well-received.

In the end she came and sat down at the table opposite
him and placed her hands carefully on the surface.

'Do you see what I am getting at?'

Given that she hadn't spoken for some three or four
minutes, he replied that he couldn't.

'It's a set-up, Doug.'

'What do you mean?'

'Do I have to spell it out? You were unexpectedly released
from prison. There was no one to meet you because no one
had been told about this new development. But "Hey diddle
diddle," a good Samaritan turns up, tells you the bus has
broken down — I bet it hadn't — and through the goodness
of his heart offers to give you a lift. But he never gets to his
alleged destination — Oxford — because he is dramatically
rerouted to Aylesbury, so unexpectedly that he has to dump
you in the middle of the countryside before driving off into
the distance. And you, Mullen, find yourself located exactly
where they want you to be at the very time they want you
there, close to where the next body will be found. And no
doubt something connecting you to the poor woman's death
will be found on her.'

'I'm more concerned about Becca. After all, I'm home
now.'

But Holden wasn't listening. She was on her phone,
ringing the bus company. A few sharp questions later, she
terminated the call.

'And?' Mullen queried.

Holden ignored him, opened the door and went outside. Then she uttered a scream of such intensity that he stood rooted to the spot. That was all he needed, Holden going into meltdown. Even Rex trotted to the open door and stood there looking out, uncertain how to react. He only moved when she came striding back inside. 'A tyre blew out on the X38. Maybe I have an overactive imagination. Maybe it's these flipping drugs. Maybe I am going to end up mad as a hatter.'

'It was a good idea,' Mullen said, 'but the fact remains that Becca is missing. In that case, if she has been abducted . . .' The alarm in his voice was evident.

'Stop it, Doug,' she snapped. 'I need you to get focused and think. What are the facts? Becca drugged me. I thought at first this was just for my own good, but maybe she also wanted me to have a really good sleep while she did what she had to do. Another fact: she left the house early. Why? She was due to pick up the medication from Leo mid-morning when he had got hold of it, but she never did. So what was she doing before that? Whatever has happened to take her off-grid must have transpired during that interval.'

Mullen said nothing. He had just picked up another biscuit, but he never got it to his lips because the fraught silence that followed Holden's rant was interrupted by a single sharp beep from his mobile. He strode over and put the phone to his ear, listening intently. 'Voice message,' he rasped after a few moments. 'Maybe it's Becca.'

'Put it on loudspeaker,' she snapped, now in full boss — and bossy — mode.

'It's me.' The voice was unquestionably Becca's. 'Are you being let out? If so, thank God for that. But when?'

Holden had moved over to stand by Mullen, as if fearful of missing something vital.

'I've got your beloved detective inspector here — in my bed!' There was a giggle. 'Poor woman's not well, actually. Broke out of the psychiatric hospital. Very resourceful, I must

163

say. Anyway, she's taken refuge with me, and I am having to get some more pills to keep her stable. Actually, I've given her a double dose with her breakfast, so she'll sleep while I'm out. If she thinks she can outwit me, she's got another thing coming. Anyway, looking forward to seeing you, whenever that is. In the meantime, I'm off out to hunt the cat, before I meet Leo to get those pills for the lovely inspector.' There was a pause, then a final two words uttered in a croaky voice. 'Love you!'

Mullen was silent, embarrassed by some of what Becca had said about Holden. But Holden was totally focused on the task, nothing else. 'What time was the message?' she snapped.

'7.53 a.m.'

'And what do you think she meant when she said she was off to "hunt the cat?"'

Mullen frowned. 'The woman I met in the pub. Kat with a "K," as in Katherine, or Katerina or whatever. We talked about how we might track her down, but how could she do that?'

'Julie Baxter had a diary,' Holden said, jumping to her feet. 'Details of her appointments and customers. Krystyna had it, but she gave it to Becca.'

'What?'

'Or maybe she gave her a copy. I don't know. But we need that list, and the only person who can help us with that, as far as I can see, is Krystyna.'

'But we have no idea where she is.'

'I'll ring the office. Speak to Andy Kingston or, failing him, McPherson. They both hate me, but what the hell.'

'They'll drag you back to hospital.'

She shrugged. 'Promise me you'll visit. OK, don't promise me anything. Just give me your blooming phone. My battery is pretty much flat.'

He passed it over to her.

The problem was that she couldn't remember any of their numbers. So she rang her own. The chances were that

Kingston would have promoted himself to her office and would be sitting in her chair, preening himself. Or if not, surely someone else would pick up when they heard her phone ringing.

No one picked up. She didn't bother to leave a message. She tried the number again. The same result. 'Just one more try,' she announced to Mullen, and called a third time. This time someone picked up almost immediately.

'Are you ringing for Detective Inspector Holden?' a voice said.

'No, I *am* Detective Inspector Holden.'

There was a sudden intake of breath.

'Is that you, Jim?' She could hear the noise of muffled conversation in the background.

'Yes, this is DC Royce. Where are you? Krystyna is in all sorts of trouble for helping you escape.'

'Where is she now?'

'She's not here.'

'Is she in the office?'

'No. Look, ma'am, you have to return to the hospital. You're not well. I'll tell you what, if you give me your address, I'll get someone to pick you up.'

'Krystyna is not answering her phone. Pass me on to Andy or the chief super. That's an order!'

Time froze. Royce was talking again, but it was to someone else, and she couldn't make out what he was saying.

'Royce!' she snapped. 'Did you hear me?'

'You are suspended, ma'am, and as such you cannot give me orders. I am required to ask you where you are so that we can arrange safe transport to the hospital. My colleague has just checked your mobile number and it has come up as belonging to Mr Douglas Mullen. Are you at his house?'

'I am,' she conceded. There seemed no point in denying it. 'But I am very concerned that Detective Constable Wozniak is not answering her phone. She might be in danger.'

'I can help you with that. She is in danger of dismissal. She has been suspended for assisting you in escaping from hospital and passing on police information to inappropriate people. She has had to hand in her mobile phone and is currently at Thames Valley headquarters.'

'Whatever she did, she did at my specific request.' Holden was pleading, though quite why she was begging Jim Royce of all people, she had no idea.

'Goodbye, ma'am,' Royce said. 'Thank you for calling.' The line went dead.

* * *

'The little bastard.' Holden had turned the speaker on, so Mullen had heard everything. 'Who the hell does he think he is? Talking to you like that.'

'It doesn't matter,' she replied in a tone that killed the subject dead.

Mullen paused, realizing a change of tack was required. 'I'm sorry about Krystyna.'

'Krystyna is safe, Doug. She hasn't been abducted or stabbed or bludgeoned to death. For now she's safe. It's your Becca I'm worried about.'

'She'll be back soon, surely. She's just checking a few people out and—'

'Bloody hell, Doug, get a grip. She's not answering her phone.'

'Nor was Krystyna.'

Holden stared at him. Her eyes seemed huge. It was hard not to think of her as demented. But when she spoke, her voice was frighteningly calm. It bore no hint of the fury she was reputed to be capable of. 'You're in denial, Doug. Let us consider the facts. Julie was brutally killed, in what may or may not have been a sexually motivated attack. Our second victim was killed with an overdose of drugs. But no severe beating. She was dumped or killed very close to your house, in a place where you walk your dog. And she was wearing a green coat that you recognized as identical to the one worn by the woman in the pub. That looks to me like a deliberate

166

attempt to put you in the frame for murder. Are you with me so far?'

Mullen nodded.

'Victim three was killed in a brutal but somewhat different assault. And the killer seems to have hoped to pin the murder on Becca, since you were still in prison. That's three different MOs. Whatever else it might be, to me that doesn't look anything like the work of a traditional serial killer.'

She paused, and again Mullen nodded. He could feel the anxiety rising in him like a wild stallion gone loco.

'So, here's my theory.' She paused, gathering her breath. 'It's personal, Doug. It's about you. It's about getting you locked up for murder, and if that hasn't worked so far, then the killer's next step could well be to kill Becca and try and pin it on you.'

Mullen swore under his breath.

'So who the hell might want to see you locked up in prison for murder?'

'I suppose there might be several people whose marriages I have screwed up by spying on one or other of them.'

'But there's no one who stands out, someone who threatened to kill you when they discovered your part in it?'

'No.' Mullen felt his world collapsing around him. If Becca died, after all they had been through, and all because of him . . .

'It's my fault,' Holden said suddenly. 'You're going to hate me, Doug. I told Krystyna to give Julie Baxter's diary to Becca. She and I had both been squeezed out of the investigation, so I thought maybe Becca could help if she saw the diary.'

'Damn you, Susan!' For a moment Mullen wanted to grab her and shake the hell out of her, but when he saw the distraught look on her face, he paused, and then to his astonishment his legs gave way beneath him and he collapsed onto the floor like a sack of potatoes. He began to wail. 'If she's found the killer, she's got no idea how to defend herself. She's probably dead already.'

167

Mullen's defeatism was like a red rag to Holden's inner bull. She moved from distraught to furious in the blink of an eye. 'Douglas Mullen, don't you dare talk about Becca like that. If she can't fight herself out of a corner, then I'm not the craziest bitch in the Thames Valley Police force. And if you're going to give up on her and lie on the floor crying like a baby, you'll never forgive yourself. Pull yourself together. Maybe the actual diary is somewhere here in the house. She might have written down the people she wanted to visit on a separate piece of paper.'

'Why?'

'Because the diary is evidence. She knows it will have to be handed back. She will know that if she lost or destroyed it or even underlined in it the people she identified, it would be very damaging to you and might make it more likely that you — and she — would be prosecuted for murder.'

Mullen swallowed, fighting back his despair.

'On your feet, soldier,' she yelled. But she didn't wait to see him obey because she was storming up the stairs like a crazed antelope. 'I'll start with her bedroom.'

Mullen looked around. He went to the pegs and rifled through the pockets of her various coats. Then his own coats (he only had two). He pulled out the third drawer down to the left of the sink. This was where the various instruction booklets were kept, but it took him only seconds to realize that there was no diary hidden there. He glanced around the room, in the hope that something would catch his attention, but nothing did.

Upstairs he could hear Holden talking and shouting to herself — or maybe to some internal persecutor. He had better go and help before she went completely haywire. But when he got to Becca's bedroom, he found he was too late. Holden was on her knees tugging wildly at the bottom drawer of the big chest of drawers. The other drawers were all missing, tossed aside on the floor. Their contents had been strewn across the bed.

'What the hell are you doing?'

Even as the words came out of his mouth, he realized they were the stupidest he could have come up with, and were pretty high risk too. *Don't poke a wasps' nest with a stick.* The words of one of his mother's neighbours jumped into his brain too late. Holden was still on her knees but glaring at him.

'I'm effing well doing something, Doug. I'm searching Becca's bedroom in the quickest way I know how.'

'But, the mess!' It was another idiot sentence.

'You can tidy it up later if you want, but right now help me. This bloody drawer is jammed.'

Suddenly, Rex barked. He had been notably silent so far, but finally he seemed to understand the urgency and the excitement of the situation. He jumped up on the bed, seized a pair of Becca's knickers in his mouth and began to shake them.

Mullen gave up all resistance. He got down next to Holden, grabbed the drawer, pushed it in, shook it as best he could and then wrenched it out. It slid out so easily that he lost his balance.

'On the bed,' Holden ordered, so he tipped it out just as she had. Yet more clothes tumbled out, but a desperate scrambling through the pile quickly revealed that there was nothing resembling a diary there.

Holden straightened up. She was panting hard, but she was on full alert, her eyes scanning the room. 'Next door!' she snapped, and before Mullen could intervene she was out on the landing and thrusting her way into the other bedroom.

'It's the baby's room,' he yelled, following her in.

'It's a shrine,' she yelled back as she grabbed hold of the Winnie the Pooh knob on the child's wardrobe and yanked the door open.

'Susan, you can't! You mustn't throw all the baby's things around. If you do, Becca'll kill me.' Yet another stupid thing to say. It was as if stupidity had taken up residence in his brain and had lined up on the parade ground of his voice box a range of idiotic sentences, each ready for immediate deployment.

'What do you take me for?' Inside the cupboard, she was sifting her way through the little shelves, her hands deftly feeling beneath and around and among the tiny clothes, bedding, nappies and other baby paraphernalia.

'Well don't just stand there,' she said. 'Keep looking.'

He looked around the room. The only other place to search was the cot. He moved over and stared down at it, all immaculately neat. *Immaculately neat?* Those were not words he associated with Becca. At home she was a bit of a scruff. Something had changed since he made his ill-fated visit into Alice's room and provoked a storm of fury from Becca. There was a baby's sleeping suit lying on top of the sheet. It seemed incongruous, ghoulish even, a terrible insight into Becca's internal trauma. He leaned over the cot and touched the suit. It was so soft and inviting and yet so deeply terrible. He wanted to cry again, to howl in grief at her loss of Alice and now, he felt sure, his loss of Becca. He picked the suit up gently, as if it were a baby, and hugged it to himself. It was heavier than he expected, as if the suit contained an imprint of the baby it should have contained.

'Doug!' Holden's voice was soft, yet there was no hint of sadness in it. Quite the opposite. She sounded excited. But then, Mullen told himself, she was seriously unwell. This wasn't the real Susan Holden. Not that he really knew who the real Susan Holden was.

'Please,' she said. She took the suit away from him and tipped it upside down over the cot. And there, onto the white sheet, fell a red diary. Holden picked it up and opened it. 'Bingo. Douglas Mullen, you really are good.'

* * *

'You know her best, Doug. How do you think she would have gone about it?'

'Why don't we try and follow in her footsteps,' he said. They were hunched over the diary on the kitchen table. He was doing his best to concentrate, and the mania that had overtaken Holden appeared to have subsided. 'She would presumably have worked her way through the diary from January, and made a list of the names and addresses of anyone who might have called herself Kat with a "K" or a "C." So Catherine, Katie, Kathleen even. My mum had a friend called Kathleen.'

'So let's do that.'

And they did, very methodically, Holden writing, Mullen calling out the details. When they reached Catherine Mead, Holden wrote it down, but drew a circle round it. 'We know she visited her the other day.'

'Do you?'

'Some busybody took a photograph of her car because she parked illegally outside Catherine Mead's house, after which the poor woman was murdered.'

'What do you mean?'

Holden ignored the question. 'So who is the next Catherine or whatever, Doug?'

He identified two more.

'Stop. Let's ring them.'

'Shouldn't we keep looking for a few more?'

'We've started to repeat the names, Doug. There may be some new clients, but if we are working the same way Becca did, then the best thing we can do is see if either of these two have been visited by her, and if so, when. After that we can decide what to do next. Let's start with the woman after Catherine Mead.'

The woman who answered had a strong Mancunian accent. Yes, someone called Becca had called earlier that morning. They had had a cup of tea together, but she had rather rushed off.

That seemed convincing, so Holden plunged on with the next person, who turned out to be a writer of romances. 'I have two different pen names,' she told Holden in a manner that indicated that she rarely admitted this to people she encountered over the phone. 'I found Julie such a time-saver. She could pop in and do my hair and be gone, and then I could push on with my latest book. Becca came at about 10.30 a.m. I think. She seemed nice enough, but looking at her own hair, I didn't feel a great deal of confidence that she would be right for me. I have a public face, so the way my hair looks is very important to me.'

Holden curtailed the phone call. For a "busy, busy writer," as she called herself, this Catherine seemed very happy to talk.

'Who else?' she said, but Mullen frowned.

'We are back with the same people and repeat appointments. We could try the ones before Catherine Mead.'

'Your turn.'

Mullen rang but got no joy. Someone who called herself Kate, who said she never let strangers in, so no she hadn't seen anyone calling herself Becca. She admitted that a rather fat woman had come and rung furiously on her bell two or three days earlier, but, 'if you're saying she's a hairdresser, then frankly I don't believe you. She was wearing a dress the size of a tent. I thought maybe she wasn't very well.'

Holden snatched the diary from Mullen. She scrutinized the pages, one after another, tapping the table impatiently with the fingers of her left hand as she did so. And then she stopped, her fingers still and silent. 'Look.' She stabbed her finger at an entry in the diary. 'Kitty. Like a cat. Do you think . . . ?'

Mullen didn't answer, or even think. He grabbed his phone again and punched in the Oxford number. He put it on loudspeaker and held his breath. Holden gently took the phone from his hand. A woman's voice would be less threatening. It began to ring. Three, four times, and then someone picked up.

'Hello?' It was a woman.

'I wonder if I might speak to Kitty? Or does she still call herself Kat?' Holden was doing a surprisingly good impression of a posh upper-middle class accent, albeit slightly over the top. 'I am an old friend of hers. I am attending a conference at the university here, and I was hoping I might be able to see her today or tomorrow.'

'She busy. Sorry,' the woman said. The line went dead.

'What do you think? Worth a try, Susan?'

'Definitely.'

'Boars Hill address.'

'As a matter of interest, and speaking not as a police officer, you don't happen to have a firearm in your possession, do you?'

He shook his head.

'That is a very great shame,' she said. 'You never know when one might come in useful.'

CHAPTER 12

She was lying in darkness, amid the distinctive reek of chloroform. Maybe some of it had impregnated her clothing, maybe it was lingering on her skin and hair. All she knew was that she could still smell it, and that she had a headache, and that her hands were behind her back, tied together with something that cut into her wrists. She thrust herself up into a sitting position and remained very still, listening. Where was she? Where was the man who grabbed her? How on earth would anyone find her? She should have left a note, clearly written "Going to X and Y and Z," — but, idiot that she was, it hadn't occurred to her to do anything so obvious. She had been focused entirely on finding Mullen's mysterious Kat, and she hadn't given a thought to what she would do if she actually found her.

She held her breath so she could hear more clearly, but the silence around her was suffocating. Then she heard a scratching somewhere behind her? A mouse? No, something a bit bigger. A rat? She shivered at the thought. Suppose it came to investigate her. Suppose it bit her. Suppose . . . she tried to suppress her anxiety, telling herself to keep calm. *Try to focus on survival. If you don't, sooner or later he'll kill you, just like he killed the others. Think positive. Maybe the police will come and rescue you? Or Doug!* Althea Potter had heard that the police were getting cold feet about him, unable to find enough evidence to convict him. Maybe he had been let out. Surely he would rescue her. He had done it once before, so why shouldn't he do it again? She shook her head. *Don't be an idiot! There is no knight in shining armour riding to your rescue. You are on your own.* Apart, of course, from the half-crazed Susan, who she had double dosed to keep her quiet.

She froze. There was another noise. The scratching had stopped. This was more of a moan, a grunt. There was some-one else in the room.

* * *

'For crying out loud, Doug, put your foot down! Bugger the speed limits.'

Mullen didn't respond. He already was driving over the speed limit, but not so fast that a bored traffic cop might decide to flag him down and read him the riot act. The last thing he wanted was to be delayed unnecessarily. And besides, if they were pulled over and the officer recognized that his travelling companion was none other than a well-known psychotic detective inspector who had absconded from a psychiatric hospital, it would only complicate matters.

He was pushing 60 on the 50 mph stretch between Benson and Shillingford, but when they had to slow down for the roundabout and the 30 mph zone in the village, he could feel Holden's stress levels rising to dangerous levels.

'Doug!' she squealed in frustration. There was a tractor in front, with a huge load of straw on a trailer behind, and it was going along at the sort of speed that frustrates even the most mild-mannered of drivers.

Mullen dropped two gears, hit the accelerator and willed his long-suffering jalopy past the tractor as fast as it would go. His engine screamed in complaint — but he was in front now, and not a police car anywhere in sight.

'Why don't you buy yourself a decent car?' she snarled. 'You're a private detective, aren't you, or are you planning to apply for a new career as a hearse driver?'

Mullen allowed himself a slight grin. They were now clear of the village and on a wide piece of carriageway and — despite the warning signs saying how dangerous this particular stretch of road was — Mullen wound his car up to 70 mph.

'That's more like it,' Holden said.

'What's the plan when we get there?'

'How the hell should I know? How about I give the orders and you follow them. We work separately, but in cahoots. Agreed?'

He nodded, reckoning that now was not the time to discuss the details, largely because there were none. She would be making things up on the hoof. No time to debate or disagree. Have a plan and go for it.

Holden fell silent for a minute or more, as Mullen squealed round the Berinsfield roundabout and wound his car up again. She was fiddling with his phone, oblivious to the bikers and their bikes lined up at the café on the left.

'You lived in Boars Hill once, didn't you?' she said suddenly.

'House-sat for a professor.'

'So you know where the Youlbury scout camp is?'

'Yes.'

'That's the road you want. After you come off the Foxcombe Road, the house is around 800 or 900 metres on the right. That'll get us there — unless, of course, this heap of rusty metal doesn't grind to a halt on Hinksey Hill.'

Mullen said nothing. He couldn't even summon up a smile. The closer they got, the more on edge he felt. Getting there would be the moment of truth. If Becca was nowhere to be found, he wasn't sure how he would react. And if she was dead, he'd probably end up in the same psychiatric ward as the crazy woman sitting in his passenger seat.

'We'll get the bastard,' Holden said, as if reading his mind. 'We'll save Becca and we'll find that poor woman you met in the pub too. And whatever happens, don't worry about me. I don't matter. I'm just a demented bitch that no one will miss.'

Mullen opened his mouth to say something, but she shut him up. 'Now, focus, Doug. The time for talking is over.'

He nodded and concentrated on the road in front. The silence was like a sledgehammer, driving home the reality of what lay ahead. It was only Holden's madness that had been keeping him sane. 'Focus, focus, focus!' he told himself.

* * *

'Your impetuosity will be the death of you!'

His father had said this more than once, but who was he to talk? It was a case of like father, like son. Look what had happened to him after a bad night at the poker table — catapulted through the windscreen of his souped-up Jaguar because he was so desperate to get home that he hadn't had the sense to fasten his seat belt.

Maybe his father had been right. Maybe he had passed his impetuosity on to his son. It was all falling apart. He never intended it to be like this. It had just happened, one thing after another. If that Julie hadn't provoked and teased him. If he hadn't seen Mullen talking to her outside the cinema. If the stupid bitch Ngung hadn't got pregnant and above herself, not to mention encouraging Kat to go out in his absence and meet that bloody private detective. If Becca hadn't tracked down Kat. If, if, if.

He hated Mullen because Becca had preferred him. What did he have to offer her? He was sleeping on her sofa for crying out loud. No house, a job that wasn't a real job, a working-class man going nowhere. How could she not see that he was a waste of space? Whereas he himself could offer her a much more comfortable life.

What now? The game was up, because Becca knew the truth. Which meant that if he let her go, he would be facing a life in prison. He had reached the endgame. He knew that, and that he was now in an extremely tricky position. There was no slick move that he could play that would transform the outcome, and yet there was no way he was going to concede victory. Throughout his life, he had lost out too many times, times when it most mattered. If he couldn't win, he could at least have his revenge. That would be a victory in itself because it would deprive

Mullen of the happiness he craved. If he himself couldn't have Becca, then neither would that bastard.

It was, ultimately, Becca's own fault that it had all come to this. She had chosen that no-hoper over himself. Even when Mullen was in custody, lined up for a lifetime behind bars, she had thrown in her lot with him, tracking down Kat through that bloody Julie's hairdressing diary, spending ages talking to that disgusting man pretending to be a woman. It made his stomach turn. So, once he had entered his house and seen the fear in the creep's eyes, there had been no option but to silence him for good.

Everything had spiralled out of control, and now there was only one move he could make. It wasn't the end he had planned for. That was the problem. He hadn't had a grand strategy. He could see that now. It had just happened. He had seen that Mullen fellow with Julie, and after that it had been a procession of events, one thing leading inexorably to another. His only hope now was to deal with Becca as swiftly and kindly as he could, and try yet again to lay the blame at Mullen's feet. As for his mother, medication would keep her out of it for as long as necessary, and once things had settled down, he would help her slip away. A trip down the stairs, or a fall into the swimming pool — easy enough to arrange an accident. Easy enough to make Lily the fall guy if one was needed. Who was going to think that it was anything except an accident? 'Poor old Kitty,' people would say. And 'Poor old Leo.'

* * *

Becca sat very still and listened again. Nothing. He had gagged her, so she couldn't speak, but she could grunt, so that's what she did. A low grunt like a pig. She waited. Had she imagined it? Was she going crazy? Was she grunting at a ghost?

Then she heard another, answering sound — this was more of a soft moan. Definitely not a rat or any other small creature. Someone else was locked in there with her. She twisted herself out of her sitting position and up onto her knees. It wasn't just her hands that were tied, her ankles were too. The only way of moving was on her knees. She began to edge towards where the noises were coming from, one short shuffle of a knee followed by a short shuffle of the other one. The floor was hard, concrete she suspected, and her knees were not slow to complain. Even so, she got into a steady rhythm and was beginning to feel confident when a sharp pain ripped through her left knee. She keeled over and squealed into her mask. But she had no intention of giving up. She eased herself back onto her knees. Through the darkness, she could hear sound again, a gentle three-note hum. It felt like an encouragement and a guide, so she hummed back, and pressed forward again, trying to ignore the throbbing in her knee.

How long it took she had no idea, but suddenly she realized that the humming was actually very close. Another shuffle and her thigh was touching her fellow prisoner. She stopped, breathing heavily through her nose. Kat — for Becca had decided by now that it must be the woman she had met in the kitchen, the woman who had met Mullen in the pub and called herself Kat — uttered a soft mewing noise through her nose. Becca paused, uncertain what to do next. When Kat touched her stomach, she jumped in surprise, but Kat didn't appear to notice, her hands slowly feeling their way up Becca's body. Over her breasts they went. In another situation this might have felt intrusive or sexually titillating, but Becca felt hugely comforted by the fact that she wasn't alone. The woman's hands reached her face, and paused there, her fingers tracing the lines of her cheeks, temples and forehead. Kat's hands were tied like her own, but whereas her own had been tied behind her, Kat's were clearly tied at the front. Was that because the killer saw her as less of a threat than Becca? It certainly gave her more freedom.

Becca nodded her head encouragingly — or so she hoped — as Kat's fingers moved over her face. And when they finally reached her gag, she nodded all the more. As Kat took a grip of the gag, Becca uttered a series of squeaks, encouraging her to have a go. With a huge grunt, Kat pulled down on the gag and suddenly she was free.

'Thank you, thank you,' she whispered. 'Are you Kat? I am Becca.'

Kat nodded and grunted, which Becca took to be a "yes."

* * *

The house was at the end of a long drive, which curved to the left before revealing an impressively large residence separated from the rest of the world by imposing wooden gates and tall stone walls. Mullen brought his car to a halt and they got out. They looked around for security cameras. They were almost certainly there somewhere, but if so they were also well-hidden. There were a couple of bird boxes. Maybe they were in those. They approached the right-hand gatepost, noting the "Friends" and "Tradesmen" bells. Holden didn't pause, pressing first one and then the other. No voice came over the intercom, and the gates remained resolutely closed.

'Time for plan B,' Holden said. 'Call 999. Say you've heard gunshots and there is an injured woman on the drive of this house.' She had earlier taken charge of his mobile phone and now handed it back. 'Then scout round and see if you can scale the wall anywhere.'

'What are you going to do?'

'I am going to complete the other part of plan B,' she said cryptically.

Mullen began to walk clockwise while he made the call. He reported Holden's lie to the call handler with all the verve of an amateur dramatics actor who has had a drink to give himself Dutch courage, panting to give it extra authenticity. While he talked, he kept his eyes on the wall and the trees nearby, searching in vain for a place where he might be able to climb up and over into the grounds of the big house. There was a large horse chestnut tree whose branches stretched out towards the wall. If he climbed up the lower, rather tricky part of the trunk, then there was a reasonable chance that he could clamber along one of those branches and jump onto the top of the wall. He tried not to think any further than that stage of the operation. Instead he focused on the tree, inspecting it more closely for the best way to complete his task. It looked most promising at the back of the tree, but his attention was wrenched away by the sound of Holden violently revving his car. He looked back and saw her reversing it back up the slope of the drive. *Where the hell was she going?*

A moment later he got his answer, though it wasn't one that he liked. The car came to an abrupt halt at the top of the slope where the drive plateaued out. Very briefly, there was an eerie and unsettling silence. This was shattered as the car's engine rose to a greater crescendo of noise. Mullen abandoned all interest in tree climbing while he witnessed what was unfolding. And then — *what the fuck!* — the car was hurtling forward towards the gate, engine squealing, gravel spitting out from under the wheels. Holden herself was hunched down low behind the wheel, eyes fixed to the front. Mullen could see her mouth open as she bellowed some sort of war cry that only she could hear.

'Stop!' he yelled, in vain. She would never hear his call, and even if she had, he knew there was absolutely zero chance of her heeding it. He watched in horror — and with a sneaking admiration for her crazy recklessness — as the car torpedoed into the gate. Mullen began to run. If plan B had been to destroy the gate, it had succeeded pretty well, but the car itself was wedged in the middle of the entrance, half hidden by a thick pall of black smoke. God only knew what sort of condition Holden was in. He ran faster, conscious that there were flashes of fire amid the smoke. Whatever else, they had now lost all chance of using surprise. If Becca was somewhere in the property and the murderer was on the premises, the danger to her had increased dramatically. *She might already be dead!* He tried to dismiss the thought. She wasn't a woman to give in. Becca was a survivor.

When he reached the car, he wrenched open the driver's door, thrust his arms into the smoke and grabbed Holden.

Stupidly, she hadn't put on her seat belt. Very stupid indeed when you are planning a ram raid on a extremely solid wooden gate, but it meant that when he pulled at her there was nothing to hold her in the seat. They both of them ended up on the ground, choking and coughing.

'Leave me!' she screamed. Her face was blistered and her hair had been scorched to nothing. 'For crying out loud, find Becca!'

* * *

He ignored the insistent ringing of the bell, hoping against hope that they would give up and go away, but of course they didn't. When your luck has run out, that is what happens. He waited, monitoring the cameras to see what they would do next. He recognized Mullen, and the woman — hell, it was that wretched detective inspector. Mullen had started to look for a way of getting over the wall, whereas she had got in the car and was reversing back up the drive. Was she leaving? Going to get reinforcements? Or what?

Moments later he got his answer, as she accelerated back down the drive and straight into the gates. The loud bang and a cloud of smoke shook him into action.

* * *

Mullen got up from the ground and took a final look at Holden. He felt guilty leaving her here in such a state. God only knew how long it would take for the paramedics to turn up. But there was little he could do practically. He could offer her moral support, but that was all. Becca might still be alive.

'I'll find her, Susan, don't you worry.' Silly words of comfort and confidence, but that is what people do some-times. After all, saying something, anything, is better than nothing.

He slipped between the car and the gatepost. Only now did he get a proper view of the house, which was big and

182

modern, but he had no time to admire it. He headed straight for the front door, which was locked. He battered on it with his fist, but he didn't expect — or get — an answer. He moved on, skirting the house, searching for another way in and peering through various windows as he passed them. He saw no one. When he reached the back door, he found that locked too. No one was going to let him in.

He looked around and spotted something that immediately caught his fancy, a marble statuette of a naked Greek woman a metre or so high. He went and picked it up. It was heavy and beautifully smooth, and for a very brief moment he felt guilty about what he was going to do with it. From the front of the house, he could hear Holden suddenly scream in pain. He turned, ran to the long window immediately to the right of the back door and smashed the statuette hard into the glass. It exploded spectacularly.

Moments later, he was inside. He ran along the short corridor and found himself in a huge modern kitchen, all silver and grey and high-class utensils. Not that he was bothered about its style. Like all classy modern kitchens, there was a wooden knife block on one of the work surfaces, offering him a choice of no less than seven knives. He grabbed the one in the middle. If he encountered the killer now, he would at least have a chance.

'Aagh!' The scream came from a woman cowering in the corner, half hidden by a tall houseplant on a wooden stand. She was holding her hands either side of her face, as if traumatized by what was going on around her, and perhaps especially by the fact that there was a strange man with a very sharp kitchen knife staring at her. Mullen was reminded of Munch's *The Scream*.

'I won't hurt you,' he said. 'But tell me, where are they?'

Her mouth opened, but then it shut again.

'I am looking for a woman called Becca,' he said. 'And someone called Kat?'

'Go,' she said. 'Go!'

'Go where?'

'Too late for that.' It was a man's voice. A familiar one too. Mullen turned and saw Leo Francombe standing in the doorway at the back of the room. He was holding a shotgun, casually, but pointed in the general direction of Mullen. 'Put the knife down, Doug. I won't ask you twice.'

Mullen put the knife on the work surface. 'Have you killed Becca?'

'Put these on.' Francombe moved forward and slid a pair of handcuffs across the large round table that separated the two of them.

'Where is she?'

'I'll give you five seconds, then I pull the trigger.'

Mullen knew he had no option. All he could do was delay matters, and hope that the police turned up before Francombe killed him. He picked up the handcuffs and clipped them onto his wrists. Click, click! The die was cast.

'Kill me if you like, Leo, but not Becca. She's had one hell of a time.'

He laughed. 'Killing you is exactly what I intend to do, Doug. I want to punish her. I offered her everything, and she turned me down. You know why? Because of you. She chose you rather than me.'

'You failed her when she most needed you,' Mullen said. He had to engage him, distract him, buy whatever time he could. 'When Alice was born . . .' He let the words hang.

'It was you she asked for.' He spat the words out. 'Even though it wasn't yours—'

'It? The baby was a she. Alice was a she!' Mullen was losing control, but he was past caring. 'I held her in my arms until she had gone cold and the nurse insisted on taking her away, while Becca lay traumatized on the bed. Where the hell were you then?'

'Shut up!' Francombe screamed. 'Or I'll blow your head off now.'

Mullen shut up. Pushing Francombe over the edge was not a good idea.

'Lily!' Francombe called across the room towards the woman still cowering in the corner. She moved hesitantly towards him. 'Lead him down!' he snapped, his eyes — like his double-barrelled shotgun — still trained on Mullen. 'Follow her. Don't try to grab her or use her as a shield, because if you do I'll kill you both. And so far she has done nothing to deserve that.'

Lily led the way down a flight of stairs, Mullen a couple of steps behind her. At his back, he could sense the ominous presence of Francombe — on edge and unpredictable.

'Hold the door open,' Francombe commanded. For a few milliseconds Mullen considered the possibility of wrenching it away from the woman and slamming it shut behind him, but the plan disintegrated before it was even half formed. Even without handcuffs, it would have been a ridiculously high-risk strategy.

Mullen stared into the pitch dark of the room, and heard the click of a switch behind him. In the sudden harsh light, he saw two women, huddled in the corner — Becca and Kat. He felt a surge of relief.

'Becca,' he called out. He felt a stab of pain in the back of his head as Francombe thrust the muzzle of his gun into it. He tripped and fell forward, his face striking the surface of the floor.

'Up on your knees, Muggins.'

'Ignore him,' Becca yelled, as if calling him a stupid name was the worst Francombe could do to him.

'Are you OK, Becca?' Mullen called, expecting another blow. It didn't come.

'On your knees, I said!'

Mullen did his best to push himself up. His main concern now was to delay and distract Francombe. 'Leo,' he said calmly, 'you do realize the police will be here soon? They know all about you. For your sake, I strongly advise you to put your weapon down. Maybe you can plead insanity.'

'I might do that, Doug. But first I'm going to kill you.'

Becca screamed, 'For God's sake, Leo, I beg you. He's done you no harm.'

'You chose him over me, Becca. So it's you who've done him harm.'

'Leo!' Kat spat the word out like an order, in much the same way she must have spoken to him as a child, on the occasions when his behaviour had surpassed all reasonable bounds. 'You will put that gun down now!'

Francombe stared at his mother. He seemed bemused by this unexpected development — his mother telling him off. Recalling her soft-spoken manner in the Turf Tavern, Mullen was surprised too, and comforted by the fact that she was on his side. Not that he expected it to make any difference. Francombe had already killed three people, so why would he bother to stop now? Three or four, what was the difference?

'Say your prayers, Mullen. I'm going to count to five and then it will be all over for you. One . . . two . . .'

Events moved so quickly that later it was hard to piece together what actually happened. Mullen looked up at Francombe and stared him in the face. He was not going to give him the satisfaction of seeing him grovel. He heard a movement behind him. He wanted to look round, but when Francombe called out, 'Sit down, both of you,' he knew it had to be Becca and Kat, forcing themselves to their feet, refusing to be cowed. He felt hugely encouraged by that, even though he knew that their support and defiance was of no use at all. Francombe would kill him, and then maybe he would kill both of them. What about the maid, Lily? Her too?

'Three . . . four . . .' The gaps were longer now, while Francombe readied himself for what he was about to do.

'For Alice's sake, Leo, don't do this!' Becca's final plea for sanity. Mullen heard it but didn't take it in because he had spotted a movement behind Francombe. Mullen had no idea of the effort of will it must have taken for Holden to drag herself from the gate to the house. But like an avenging angel, there she suddenly was, edging down from the top of the stairs, clinging to the banister to stop herself falling. Francombe must have heard her, or sensed her presence. He turned, swinging the gun in her direction. Holden uttered a yell — or rather a battle cry — and plummeted forward. There was a sudden explosion of noise as Francombe fired one of the barrels, but Holden's downward trajectory saved her. She collided with his ankles and held onto them like she was never going to let them go. Mullen heaved himself up onto his legs and drove himself forward, looping his manacled hands over Francombe's head and yanking down and back with every gram of strength he possessed.

The shotgun clattered to the ground. Francombe struggled to snatch it up, but Mullen had the upper hand. Someone picked up the gun. Francombe gave a squeal of pain as the barrel was jammed into his face. There was another bang, and suddenly everything fell silent. 'Thank God,' Kat said. 'Thank God.'

The silence was ruptured by the welcome sound of ambulance and police sirens, belatedly but finally announcing the good news that the cavalry had arrived.

And when they did penetrate the house, they found Holden lying, arms akimbo, on the stairs, one hand gripping the shotgun and covered in Leo Francombe's blood.

EPILOGUE

Several days had passed, though Susan Holden wasn't sure how many. It was the middle of the afternoon, and she opened her eyes to see a familiar face looking down at her. It was Becca Baines. Holden tried to smile, but creasing her face was a painful process.

'How are you, Susan?'

'Alive. Feeling like shit. You know how it is, Becca.'

Baines leaned forward and squeezed her hand. 'We owe everything to you,' she said, looking her full in her blistered face and trying not to flinch.

'Don't be ridiculous.'

Baines had wanted terribly to pay a visit to Holden, but now she was here, she found she was tongue-tied. She pulled up a chair and sat down. 'I've decided to go back to work.'

'Good. And how is Doug?'

'He's buying you some treats from the shop. He'll be up in a minute.'

'Hell, Becca. I don't want treats. What I need is gossip to alleviate the tedium.'

'I didn't know you were into gossip.'

'So, for a start, what the hell is going on between the two of you? I need to know. It'll keep me sane.'

'He's moved upstairs, if that's what you mean.'

'That's exactly what I meant.'

'I'm trying again for a baby.'

'You and Doug?' Holden grimaced with pain. 'Every time you make me smile, it hurts.'

'Sorry.'

'You and him. About blooming time.'

There were footsteps behind Becca. She turned, expecting to see Mullen, but the person standing in the doorway was Krystyna Wozniak. She had a multi-coloured bag slung over her shoulder, which she dropped on the bed before leaning down and, to Becca's amazement, kissing Holden's ruined face. 'Got you a few things,' she said.

THE END

AUTHOR'S NOTE

When writing crime fiction set in and around Oxford, I have always tried to make best use of well-known (and not-so-well-known) places. When a character walks along a street and sees a shark diving into the roof of one of the houses, the chances are that the shark actually exists. If you don't believe me, take a stroll along New High Street in Headington to check it out!

In this particular story, the various real venues include the Ultimate Picture Palace and the Turf Tavern. But of course my story is a work of fiction, and so the people you come across in these places are the product of my imagination and are not real. As for the internal workings of such places, my story should in general be true to life, but I may also have included some details that are just made up!

I am writing fiction, not fact.

Peter Tickler
February 2023

THE JOFFE BOOKS STORY

We began in 2014 when Jasper agreed to publish his mum's much-rejected romance novel and it became a bestseller.

Since then we've grown into the largest independent publisher in the UK. We're extremely proud to publish some of the very best writers in the world, including Joy Ellis, Faith Martin, Caro Ramsay, Helen Forrester, Simon Brett and Robert Goddard. Everyone at Joffe Books loves reading and we never forget that it all begins with the magic of an author telling a story.

We are proud to publish talented first-time authors, as well as established writers whose books we love introducing to a new generation of readers.

We have been shortlisted for Independent Publisher of the Year at the British Book Awards three times, in 2020, 2021 and 2022, and for the Diversity and Inclusivity Award at the Independent Publishing Awards in 2022.

We built this company with your help, and we love to hear from you, so please email us about absolutely anything bookish at: feedback@joffebooks.com.

If you want to receive free books every Friday and hear about all our new releases, join our mailing list: www.joffebooks.com/contact

And when you tell your friends about us, just remember: it's pronounced Joffe as in coffee or toffee!

www.ingramcontent.com/pod-product-compliance
Ingram Content Group UK Ltd.
Pitfield, Milton Keynes, MK11 3LW, UK
UKHW042246290925
8135UKWH00003B/175